FIGHT

Kim —
Thank you so much for making me feel welcome & part of the team. Thank you for being a listening ear & always being so helpful. Thanks mostly for supporting me! XO, Jeff

FIGHTING DEMONS

T.C. Flenoid

Fighting Demons ©2008 T.C.Flenoid

All rights reserved. No part of this book may be reproduced in any form or by any means without prior consent of the owner, excepting brief quotes used in interviews.

This is a work of fiction. Any references or similarities to actual events, real people, living or dead, or real locales is entirely coincidental.

First in print: May 2011

ISBN-13: 978-1453851920
ISBN- 10: 1453851925

This is for everyone who
supports and believes in me.
I won't let you down.
This is only the beginning…

ACKNOWLEDGMENTS

All thanks to my Lord and Savior Jesus Christ from which all my talents and blessings are rendered. Mama, thank you for putting up with me asking you to read each chapter over and over… and over. Thank you Karon, for pushing me to finish a book- finally! We're making this happen, babe! My boys are my inspiration to strive for success. Bria, thanks for doing exactly what little sisters are supposed to do. ☺ Aintee, you stepped in so many times when things were rough and I owe you so much. G-mama, my guardian angel, I love and miss you. I know you're smiling down on us all. Fairs, Hykes, Williams, Boyds, Hills, inlaws… my family is my backbone. I gotta thank my 'proofreaders', Keytra, Jeek, Jess, Candance, and Nona, for giving me props and hyping me up before I was even done writing. Jeek… what can I say? Never met anybody quite like you. You're more like family. Keytra… I honestly think you might be my biggest fan! Everybody YOU know has been waiting for this! LOL! Love you! Mrs. Curran, you awakened talent in a little girl who didn't even realize it was there. I'm forever grateful for that. Thanks Ms. Catherine for my cover idea!! You know how I *stressed* over it… If I spent time with you or enjoyed your company, if you did me a favor or gave me a shoulder to lean on, you're appreciated. If I failed to mention you specifically, I know you'll be on my head soon enough. I love ya'll! This is ONLY the beginning!!!

PART ONE

lies, confusion, and lust

ONE

There I was on the floor of Reggie's musty room on his dirty mattress. Springs were poking in my thighs through the faded blue comforter. I wanted to scream when he reached for my belt, plus, he smelled like weed, as always. If I smoked maybe it would've been different. But I didn't. So basically, the boy was funky. By the time he got my bra off, I'd focused on the Aaliyah poster taped to the sickening sea foam green wall. I wasn't thinking about her, the mouse I heard squeaking in the closet, or the water bug I was pretty sure I saw scurry under the dresser. I was thinking about Aaron with his fine chocolate self. It was the fifth time I'd had sex with Reggie and each time I had thought about Aaron. It was a shame I'd picked the wrong one.

***

I met Aaron and Reggie on the same day. Theresa and I were strolling the neighborhood thinking we were cute when Reggie walked up and introduced himself. His face was smooth and dark and his smile made him handsome. Theresa thought he was ugly, but his forwardness did something for me, so I gave him my number. Later that day we saw a sexy, chocolate tenda ride past on his bike. When he looked up at us and nodded I think I got wet. We sat there gawking at him- lost in his sexiness- like a couple of idiots until he disappeared down the street.

"Now that's who you shoulda been givin' yo' number

to." Theresa got up and went to the bathroom while I wondered where the Hershey Kiss went. Not five minutes later he was riding back... and up in my grass... smiling. All I could think was, "Damn he is *foine*." I heard Theresa at the screen door giggling but I blocked her out. Mr. Hershey Kiss had come back for me. He was darker than anybody I'd ever seen and it was sexy as hell. Judging by the gym shorts and cut-off t-shirt, I figured he'd been playing football or basketball or something. His hazel eyes shone under thick eyebrows and the single gold in his mouth gleamed along with his perfect teeth.

"You gonna stand there or come down here and talk to me?" *Even his voice was sexy!* I tried to act like I wasn't phased but I know he saw through the silly look on my face.

"I'm Kyra," I managed to get out. Even though my cheeks hurt, I couldn't stop smiling.

"I'm Aaron." I looked at his arms stretching out to the handlebars. They were thick, covered in tattoos, and glistening with sweat. He got up and laid his bike down. Normally I don't like people in my grass, but this brotha was about 5'11, skinny but still muscular, with strong legs, clean braids, and a fresh lining. "I couldn't just ride past you like that." He acted like he already knew I wanted him so I just stood there and waited to see what he was gonna say next. "I saw you sittin' here and wanted to be nice and give you my number." At first I was so excited I didn't realize how damn cocky he was. I decided to just play along.

"Oh, so you're gonna be *nice*?" I teased, though I went to get a pen and paper anyway. He said he was looking forward to hearing from me. Reggie called me before I got up the courage to call Aaron so Aaron had to settle for being just a friend. I knew I wanted Aaron, but I wanted him too bad, and that scared me.

***

Reggie's irritating offbeat shaking snapped me back into

reality. I don't know how long he'd been doing whatever the hell he called himself doing. And I don't know how he could bust with me just laying there. Hell, maybe I got so used to ignoring him I learned to fake it unconsciously. He was dumb enough to fall for it too. I needed a shower...

***

Walking the five long blocks home I had time to think about how disgusted I was with so many things in my life. Reggie was one of those things. He was supposed to be my boyfriend but I couldn't stand him. The way he smelled, the way he walked and dressed, and the boy wasn't bright at all. Plus, he thought he was God's gift to women but hadn't even had the stroke to give me an orgasm. School was another one of those things. I hated it. Couldn't stand the thought of getting up before the sun came up and riding the Bi-State bus to listen to people *talk* half the day. I had better things to do with my time, but my mama threatened me. What other choice did I have? My ex boyfriend, Chris, was one of those things. He was a drug-dealing cheater and a headache I was trying my best to avoid. My child molesting father, now he was the main thing. When I was six, he was sentenced to six years for possession and armed robbery. I seriously thought about running away after he got out of jail because Mama decided to let him back in. I was ashamed to have a jail-bird father and more ashamed to have a mother desperate enough to take him back. Mama was working nights though and was happy to have somebody home with me again. I guess after six years with no sex and a woman who worked too much, in my father's eyes his 12-year-old daughter was looking pretty grown up.

When he first started sneaking in my room at night, it was only once a month. I guess he figured he'd test me to see how scared I would become of him. See if I had the balls to tell. I didn't. The past three years, it gradually escalated to once or twice a week. I hated myself staying quiet and not being able to break my mother's heart. I hated myself for hating her because she wouldn't take care of him sexually. Hated myself for holding it in for so long.

    Before I knew it I had walked my five blocks. My face was wet from a mixture of tears and sweat. My feet were cement bricks as I trudged up the front steps. It was only 4:45 so I knew Mama was a long way away from getting home. I ran right past the living room into the kitchen, the past three years heavy on my mind. I grabbed the first knife I could get my hands on.

    Returning to the living room, I saw that he was sleeping. He looked so peaceful yet, under that thick façade, I knew an evil bastard slept. I stood there staring a hole in his chest, my feet glued to the floor with indescribable fear. The handle on the knife burned the palm of my hand and I knew what I was about to do was wrong. I turned away shaking the perverted thought from my mind. I stopped abruptly at the picture near the doorway to the kitchen. All three of us, smiling as if things were perfect. *The Huxtables, The Brady Bunch...* It was all a lie, and suddenly I felt his fingers inside me, his hot liquored breath on my neck, his disgusting manhood hardening on my leg. My heart forced me to pivot back toward his chair in front of the television. I could feel 6-6-6 carving itself into the back of my neck as I begged God to stop my sinful hands from what was about to happen. I couldn't fight the urge so I prayed that He would forgive me. In the back of my mind, I heard my father's voice calling to me, threatening me. Raising the knife above my head caused my sweat glands to work overtime. Twice I had to wipe wetness from my eyes and reposition my hands.

    When he snorted and grabbed himself, a switch must've gone off in my head because my arms flew down. As the knife punctured his chest, his eyes popped open and he reached out, his massive hands wrapping around my neck. My breathing fell short at his manly grip. I tried my best to scratch at him but it didn't work so I began to shake violently, hoping I could escape him. It was no use. My eyes began to roll into the back of my head. He was making sure if he wasn't going to wake up in the morning, I wasn't either. Just as I felt myself slipping into darkness, his grip loosened and I slumped to the floor.

Moving hair from my face, I watched my molester dying, one hand on the knife in his chest, one reaching out to me. The hatred in his eyes transformed into agony before he fell forward. All I could do was shrink to the closest corner of the now enormous room, pulling my legs up to my chest and resting my head on my knees. My dry, unregretful eyes transfixed on the lifeless body and the crimson river running along the plush white carpet. It was over. I had murdered the biggest demon in my life, my father.

TWO

I didn't know how long I'd been focusing on the stain growing on the floor before I heard the knock. I pulled myself up from the floor to peep out of the blinds. Thank God it was Aaron. I swung the door open and yanked him in. He'd never been in my house and I'm sure he had other things on his mind when I pulled him in like that, but I was about to shock the hell out of him. Right there in the front hall I poured my heart out starting with the day my father got out of jail and ending with a short walk to the living room. Aaron turned quickly from the body and looked at me. I searched his eyes for forgiveness and understanding. My stare begged him, pleaded with him. The tears I began to shed were for my pain and anguish alone. I had no remorse for the asshole messing up my mama's carpet.

"We gotta come up with something to tell the police." Aaron said. Then he hugged me. At that moment I knew I loved him. He found my mama's work number on the refrigerator and called. I stood quietly in the background while he stayed discreet, only stating that there had been an accident and that I needed her to come home immediately. Then he called the police to tell them there'd been a murder. By the time the flashing lights pulled up, I'd perfected the story Aaron and I had come up with.

"My father's been raping me since he got out of jail when I was twelve. I was too scared to say anything so it went on for years until today when he came at me in the kitchen. He tried to lift up my skirt and I flipped. I grabbed a knife and told him, 'Stay away from me or I swear I'll kill you.' He laughed at me so I pointed the knife at him. He was backing up but he still acted like it was all a joke. I even thought to myself I was joking until he ended up bumping into his chair and falling in it. That's when he shoved his hand between my legs trying to pull at my panties. I stepped on his foot and he grabbed my neck. He wouldn't let go. I had to do it. I had to." Aaron was beside me rubbing my shoulder as I squeezed the tears out.

"And how did you end up here young man?" A chubby Asian, Detective Howa, turned his questioning to Aaron. His partner, Detective Jordan, a pretty black woman, seemed very sympathetic, putting a hand over mine and gripping hard.

"I came over to visit Kyra and she answered the door crying. I had to beg her to tell me what happened. She told me everything before she even let me in. I was gonna check to see if he was dead, but I looked at him and I was sure. So I called Kyra's mom then called the police." Just then I heard Mama.

"This is my house, let me in!" Then, nothing but screams. The detectives got up to join the rest of the STLPD and medical examiners in the living room. Aaron and I followed slowly. Mama and I locked eyes for a brief moment but I could read her like a book. "What the hell happened?" she was asking me. Detectives Howa and Jordan escorted my mama back towards her office where we'd been before.

"Mrs. Blasik…"

"Ms. Conner," Mama interrupted Detective Howa because she and my father had never been married.

"I'm sorry. Ms. Conner and Mr. …" he glanced at Aaron.

"Aaron Washington."

"Mr. Washington. Did either of you know before the incident that Kyra's father had been molesting her?" Aaron shook his head while Mama sank quietly into her computer chair with horror in her eyes. That didn't last long. She quickly broke the silence.

"That sick son-of-a-bitch!" Then she made a howling noise I don't think I'd ever heard before. Detective Jordan bolted in front of her to keep her from rushing into the living room.

"Ms. Conner," the female detective spoke softly. "Allegedly, Mr. Blasik has been molesting your daughter since his return from prison. My partner and I are to understand that was three years ago?" Mama looked at me, confused, hurt and pissed off. She nodded and leaned against the computer stand. "Mr. Blasik allegedly made another move on your daughter today and tried to strangle her, forcing her to protect herself." By then, Mama's face was expressionless. I couldn't tell what she was thinking and I didn't like the way the detective kept using the word *allegedly*.

"Can I get one of you in here to check the young lady's neck?" Howa called into the living room. A young, white woman with a short ponytail and cat-eye glasses entered and motioned for me to lift my chin. Aaron held my hand while the woman checked the bruises and fingerprints I already knew were there. She nodded to the detectives who were talking quietly.

"Take the prints and run 'em." Howa ordered.

"That won't be necessary." A bald man entered with a tape in gloved hands. "Found it in the cushion of his chair." I was wondering what the hell was on that tape the man held up. Mama was still shocked. She hadn't moved. The bald man stuck the tape into the player in the computer room and I broke down when I saw myself being raped by my father. The tape wasn't dated and I couldn't tell just by looking when it was. It had gotten to the point I could just go blank during sex- if you could call it that. There was no time or date when my father was in my room. Just blackness and pain. And the pervert had recorded it.

Aaron turned me away and held me while Mama finally let go and started to wail. In a ridiculous way I was relieved that there even *was* a tape. How often is it that you kill someone and that very person helps you get away with it? In my eyes though, I was the victim anyway. That bastard finally got what he deserved. It didn't take long before I felt my mama behind me mumbling her many apologies. I was almost as sorry for her as I was for myself. I never trusted that man. She, on the other hand, had loved him, trusted him, waited for him, and supported his jobless ass. In return, he'd cheated and gotten locked up. And when he did get out, he sat on his butt, ran through her hard-earned money and molested her daughter.

We made our way to the door, watching silently along with a street full of nosy neighbors, as they loaded Eric Daniel Blasik into the morgue van.

May he forever rot in hell.

***

Even though we got to the police station at around seven, it was after midnight when we left. During all the questioning, note taking and requisitioning, Mama tried to talk Aaron into going home, but he refused to leave me. Detective Jordan pulled me to the side before the night was over and gave me the number to a shrink. I took the card but, as far as I was concerned, that book was closed. I never wanted to talk about it again and I definitely didn't need therapy.

I felt free leaving the station. With the bruises on my neck, that man's skin under my nails, and the videotape, the detectives were more or less focused on ruling the murder as self defense. Mama called to get a hotel room because we both refused to sleep in the house that night. I had to convince her I wasn't traumatized and that I forgave her for being so blind. I wasn't completely sure of the latter. When she finally fell asleep, I left her a note telling her where I'd be and ran to the bus stop. In twenty minutes I was at Aaron's bedroom window. It was 3:30 in the morning and I felt crazy as hell, but what he'd done for me that night was fresh in my mind. I needed to be with him, not stuck in the bed with my mama.

It took a few knocks to get him up, but his face lit up when he saw me. He helped me into the window and hugged me tight. Words weren't needed. I pulled back and kissed him. It seemed to last forever and we both knew our feelings for each other had changed that day. I told him something no one else in my world knew. He lied to the police to cover for me.

We moved slowly, like neither of us had been waiting months for what was about to happen. He was gentle and made me feel like silk. Every kiss, every touch took me to a place I'd never imagined. I couldn't believe I, Kyra Blasik, was actually making love to *Aaron Washington*. I was damn near outdone the third time I came, and when he finally came too, I had tears running down my cheeks. I had no idea I could ever feel like that. I didn't see what happened with me and my father as sex, and Reggie had never made me cum, let alone cry. Aaron kissed me on my neck and we reminisced over the past year, how we'd flirted and kicked it on my porch. We both decided I should go back to the hotel or my mama would pass out when she woke up and realized I wasn't there. We kissed a little more before getting dressed and walking to the bus stop.

"So you know this means that nigga is out of the picture right?" I just looked at him.

"What do you think?" We kissed until the bus came. When I got back to the hotel Mama was oblivious to my having been gone. I crumpled up the letter I'd left and quietly crawled into bed. I easily fell asleep, Aaron filling my every thought.

THREE

The carpet cleaners took forever and, even though I had no regrets, it still felt awkward being back in the house. Mama took down every picture with that man in it and packed all his clothes and shoes to donate to the Goodwill. I told her we should've had a yard sale. We might as well profit from his being gone. She looked at me like I was crazy. I really didn't know if she believed the whole 'self defense' story, but if she didn't, her guilt over the entire situation kept her quiet.

I didn't know what I was gonna tell my best friends but I had to come up with something. There hadn't been any cameras or news crews at my house the night before but, judging by the numbers of curious neighbors on their porches, it was bound to get out that someone had died.

***

I'd known Theresa, Kim and Tasha since elementary school. Kim, Tasha's older sister, sort of adopted Theresa and I as her younger sisters too. I appreciated her for that. She gave me someone to confide in when I wanted a more mature point of view and couldn't talk to Mama. Being four years older than the rest of us gave her what I thought was an edge on life. Though she knew some things Theresa and Tasha didn't know about me, she still wasn't aware of what had been going on behind closed doors.

I had called Theresa and told her to meet me at Tasha's house. Kim answered the door, grinning and seven months pregnant. I smiled back wondering how she'd react to what I had to say.

"I woulda picked you up, crazy. You didn't have to walk," she joked. "Your friends are in the front room." I didn't want to go into the living room but they already knew I had something to say. Tasha was on the floor between Theresa's legs getting her cornrows redone. Kim plopped down beside them and I sat in the chair across from them. They all looked at me, waiting.

"So... what's up?" Theresa looked up from Tasha's braids. I was wondering whether I should lie or not. I decided that would be a good idea. If they knew everything I'd have to sit through the, "Why didn't you tell us?" lecture from all three of them.

"My father raped me." I finally blurted out. For a moment their mouths dropped in disbelief.

"Oh my God, Kyra, oh my God!" Kim's hormones ran out in tears as she rushed over to me. The others responded a little differently.

"That ignorant asshole!"

"Nasty, perverted bastard!"

They were amped and ready to fight. Tasha pulled her long braids back into a ponytail while Theresa continued yelling.

"Where is he Kyra?" She was popping her knuckles. "Where- the hell- is- he?"

"Calm down and stop talking so loud." Kim motioned upstairs to where she and Tasha's parents were. "Sit down and act like ya'll got some sense." She crossed in front of me and sat back down on the couch. "Tell us what happened, Kyra." Tasha and Theresa sat down side by side, hushed by Kim's anger. I wouldn't completely lie, I'd just bend the truth a little bit.

"When I got home from Reggie's house yesterday I guess my father had been drinking 'cause he started talking about how pretty I looked and how good I smelled. I tried to ignore him but he grabbed me and I screamed and tried to fight him but ya'll know how big he is." All three of them listened attentively, like I was telling a scary story at a campfire. I paused for a minute wondering if I should act like I was hurt, then decided against it. "I had on a skirt, the pink denim one. He grabbed me from the back and pushed me up against the sink."

"I know it's yo' daddy," Theresa interrupted, "but I swear to God I'll kill that muthafucka!" Tasha nodded in agreement and Kim was still full of tears.

"Too late." It was as if time stopped when I said that. I knew they had to have something to say. My friends talked a lot of crap but I knew they could never do what I'd done. They were still as frozen trees, their mouths in silent o's. "When he finished, he just got up and went to look at T.V. I took a knife out of the kitchen and... took care of him." Then I waited to see what they'd say. Theresa and Tasha were both extremely outspoken and Kim was our responsible 'mother figure.'

"Are you serious, Kyra?" Kim's eyes had dried but I could still hear the hurt in her voice. The other two sat in wide-eyed suspense. "Did you really?" she kept at it.

"Why would I up and lie like this?" I asked. Tasha and Theresa were still quiet.

"Okay then," Kim said. "Are you alright, really?"

"Honestly, I'm fine. I think he deserved it and I don't really feel bad at all. The police came and everything and ruled it as self defense after they questioned us forever."

"Yo mama was there?" Tasha cut in.

"She came home from work after Aaron called her."

"Aaron was there!" Theresa yelled.

"He came afterward and helped me calm down." I told the events of the night, purposely leaving out the video tape and the rendezvous with Aaron at three in the morning.

"How is your mama?" Kim asked.

"She's trying to cope. We sat up talking at a hotel all night. We couldn't stay at the house. But this morning she had carpet cleaners come and she took down all the pictures of him and she's probably at the Goodwill right now giving his clothes away."

"Ya'll shoulda washed and sold that shit." Tasha cut in. I tried to hold back my laughter thinking back to the same comment I'd made earlier.

"Damn, Kyra. I don't even know what to say," Theresa shook her head with a slight grin on her face. "You took care of his ass! Since you're okay I'm tempted to say I'm proud of you." Kim shot her a look of disapproval and Theresa's grin vanished. But hell, I was proud of myself. I'd taken care of a three year problem, got rid of a weed smoking probably cheating boyfriend, and fell in love in a matter of hours. Why not share my happiness?

"Me and Aaron had sex."

"WHAT?!" It was unanimous. Even Kim's sullen demeanor flickered into a smile.

"Um, can we get some details?" Tasha scooted back onto the floor like it would give her an edge over Kim and Theresa.

"I left the hotel when my mama went to sleep because I just really wanted to see him. He helped me a lot last night…"

"Yeah, I bet he did," Tasha interrupted and Kim nudged her.

"Anyway," I continued, "we talked and one thing led to another. And before ya'll even ask, yes it was firre." They all fell out laughing because they knew that was the big question.

"After you waited a year it better be." Tasha joked.

"So Kyra, how does it feel bein' a hoe?" I took a flip flop and threw it at Theresa. "I'm just sayin', last time I checked, Reggie was yo' man. So did you have sex with him yesterday too?"

"No!" I answered too fast and was too defensive. Plus, I

couldn't stop laughing. They all laughed with me. "Forget ya'll. Either way, I'm not with Reggie anymore, I'm with Aaron." Just saying his name made my heart double-dutch.

"It's about time." Kim got up and headed for the kitchen. "I got tired of watching ya'll play dumb." She disappeared up the hall. It felt good to be at ease about the day before. I needed to be around people who understood and didn't judge me. At that point I was leery about when I would return home. I didn't feel like having to look at my mama and wonder what she was thinking. Theresa was in the middle of complaining about her most recent boyfriend when she was interrupted by shattering glass and horror movie screams coming from the kitchen.

FOUR

We were tripping over each other trying to get to Kim. I could hear her parents tromping down the steps by the time we got to the kitchen. Kim was on the floor face down mumbling incoherently and Tasha along with their father helped her up. Their mother gasped, along with Theresa and I when we saw the jagged piece of glass sticking out from her stomach. Smaller shattered pieces lay where she had been.

"I fell! I tripped and fell." Kim's hands were bloody from fumbling with the glass. "Daddy…" her eyes were wide as Precious Moments as he gently lifted her up and rushed her out to the car.

"Tell her don't touch it!" their mother blurted out, tears hot on her cheeks. I hadn't noticed until we bolted out the door that Tasha was hysterical. She almost fell down the porch stairs trying to get to her father's car. Theresa and I got in the car with their mother and it was eerily quiet sitting next to her in the front seat. Her tears were a waterfall and her shirt was drenched but she made no attempt to wipe them as she followed her husband haphazardly through stop signs. I turned to look at Theresa. I knew we were both thinking the same thing. Moments ago we'd joked about death. It seemed so meaningless to us that a man had actually died by my hand. My father at that. We had just jumped from that subject to the next. Seeing Kim bleeding hadn't magically put guilt in my heart, but it made me realize I hadn't taken my actions seriously. I wasn't about to admit the truth to the police, that it wasn't self defense. If I would've stuck to the truth I would've had to go to trial and have dozens of people listening to all my embarrassing moments. Yes- it was better I lied to everyone, except Aaron of course.

Our somber party of five waited as Kim was wheeled through the huge ER doors. She had passed out on the way to the hospital and Tasha wasn't far from it. Their parents consoled each other as they tried desperately to hold back tears. I felt guilty for wondering what Aaron was doing. It was almost three, I hadn't talked to him, and I didn't want him to think I was being funny after we had sex. I wondered how my mama was- in that house by herself. What if she didn't need to be alone? I sat there trying my best to come up with reasons to get out of the hospital. I'd never seen one of my girls hurt and I hated it. I was getting a headache from trying not to scream.

It took an eternity for a doctor to come out with news. Theresa and I stood back a few feet to observe the faces of Tasha and she and Kim's parents. We couldn't hear what the doctor was saying so we grabbed hands, holding our breath until the three of them exhaled sighs of relief. My tears streamed when Tasha smiled and hugged the doctor.

My visit with Kim was brief. The baby was healthy but she was still groggy from medication. Her family needed time with her anyway. After saying my goodbyes and convincing Kim's mom I'd be fine getting home, I hopped on the bus. The AC was up way too high and I rubbed the chill bumps on my arms. I could've sworn the man behind me was talking to me. I figured he was drunk so I tried to ignore him, but he got louder and the chill bumps spread to the rest of my body.

"You- killed- me…" Forget chill bumps, I damn near froze. I seriously couldn't move. My feet were stuck to the floor and not because of the juice someone must've spilled. The voice was demonic and distorted, repeating the dreadful words over and over again. "You- killed- me… you- killed- me…"

Numbness started in my toes, and worked painstakingly through my feet. By the time the irritating tingling had worked its way to my knees, the raspy voice grew louder and I felt cracked lips on my ear. My body thawed and I jumped up and spun around. The woman behind me put her arm around a sleeping child and eyed me skeptically as I inched closer to the front of the bus. My stop was coming up anyway and I rang the bell.

There were four people waiting to get on and I waited patiently, though I was eager to get off the bus. The third person moved forward, revealing the last passenger and I shrank back. The stain on his shirt had browned and his body began to convulse violently.

"Next stop," I whispered pathetically. I turned to exit out the back and the same woman was shaking her head. She more than likely thought I was a nut case. I had a little ways to walk since I'd passed my stop. I tried to convince myself it was only because I thought Kim was on the verge of death that I was flipping out and feeling crazy. Why else would I see my father at the bus stop?

Mama was a pitiful mess. She tried to perk up when she realized I was standing in the doorway of her office. She brushed back her disheveled hair and forced a feeble smile. I wondered if I should've felt bad, if I was solely to blame for her pain. I did what I had to do and if she was in my place she probably would've done the same thing. Or maybe she would've had the courage say something...

"Hey Kyra," she came over and gave me a weak hug. "How are you doing?" Her voice was tired and frail.

"I'm okay Mama. What about you? Did you get the clothes and pictures taken care of?"

"Yeah, I had someone come and pick that stuff up. How are the girls doing?" She almost floated back down into her chair at the computer desk.

"They took Kim to the hospital to check on the baby." It

wasn't a lie, it just lacked some details. Mama just nodded her head and the phone rang. When she answered, I watched her face twist and turn and wondered who it was and why she was so agitated.

"I really don't care," she half screamed. "Well he wasn't my husband and I don't know anything about insurance." There was a long pause and I figured it had to be the morgue or some type of hospital director. "Well he wasn't my husband and I don't give a good gotdamn what you do with him! Burn him and throw his ashes in the alley with the rest of the trash." And with that, the conversation was over. It felt good to hear that I mattered more to her than he did. She may have been hurt that my father was gone, but it sure as hell hit her harder that he'd been raping me. I slid my arms around her and she started in on me again.

"You know if you would've said something I would've taken care of it." I wanted to tell her I'd taken care of it myself but I just kept my arm around her and told her I'd already forgiven her. I wasn't exactly sure if that was the truth though. Once I was upstairs, I decided I needed a long bath. I also needed to call Aaron.

"Hey, what's up," his sexy smooth voice wrapped itself around me and I almost forgot about everything and everyone else in my life.

"Nothing, missing you." I grinned, pouring too much bubble in the bath.

"I called a couple times. I thought you forgot about me. What'chu been into today?" I looked at the clock. It was almost six. How long had I been at the hospital?

"I went to see Theresa 'nem. Kim had an accident and we had to go to the hospital but she's okay and so is the baby."

"Damn, how's Tasha?" I loved the way he was concerned about my friends.

"She was a little out of it at first but when we found out

Kim was okay, she calmed down."

"That's good." I undressed while Aaron and I talked about our new relationship and teased each other about sex. The water was hot and I almost lost the phone in the bubbles so I told Aaron I'd call him back after I got out. I'd closed the blinds, turned out the lights and lit a couple of ocean breeze candles. I loved the giant tub because I could slide down and rest my head on the edge without having to bend my legs. I didn't even feel like washing up. I just wanted to soak my worries away until my fingers and toes looked like California Raisins.

Mr. Sandman was just about to bring me a dream when my bath suddenly became ice cold. I could feel the bubbles parting between my legs and I squeezed my eyes tighter thinking it was all part of my new dream. Then I heard it. The same demonic voice from the bus.

"You- killed- me…" He rose slowly at first, and then shot up until he towered over me, dripping water and covering me in Victoria Secret bubbles. I was wide-eyed with sheer panic as the permanent stain on his white t-shirt suddenly exploded. Blood soaked my hair and shot into my mouth with the taste of bitterness. I couldn't hold back shrill screams as I tried frantically to escape the bloody, never-ending waterfall. But he was tugging my hair, and then forcing me into the cold bubbles. Soapy water burned my lungs and I tried to push myself up from the floor of the tub but he was too strong. For the second time in my life I felt myself dying.

"Kyra!" Mama burst through the door, spreading a wind gust that blew out the candles. She flicked on the light switch. "You were screaming," she stammered in heavy breaths. I looked at her with bewilderment. The water was warm with pure white bubbles encircling me. My hair was drenched with bath water, not blood.

"I must've fell asleep and been dreaming," I lied. I hadn't been sleep. I'd felt everything, even the water filling my lungs as my father forced me down. Back in my room, I secretly searched for the card Detective Jordan had given me. Maybe I did need a shrink.

FIVE

Aaron was eagerly waiting with open arms. I debated on whether or not to tell him about my episodes on the bus and in the bathroom. I waited a while then decided to be brutally honest with him. He'd already shown me how well he handled my drama.

"That's normal," was all he said. I just looked at him like he was the crazy one.

"How is that normal?"

"Baby, think about what happened. No matter how much he deserved it or how tough you try to be, you feel guilty about what happened. Any normal person would. I don't wanna say it's driving you crazy, but you're probably gonna be trippin' off of it for a while." And that was that. I knew he would make me feel better and I forgot about the therapist's card lurking in my purse.

Soon my head hit the pillow, but not to sleep. Aaron was lifting me again to ridiculous heights I never even knew existed. We'd joked about our different relationships and I knew he was more experienced than I was, but none of those females mattered now. There was only me and him floating higher and higher until vibrations of ecstasy brought us back down. Lying in his arms felt so good, so right. We just lay there for a while, naked and oblivious to the world around us. I didn't want to leave and fought back tears as I boarded the bus. When I got home I called Tasha to check on Kim. She said things were still looking up and she should be home in a couple of days according to the doctor. I climbed into bed and slept peacefully without my father whispering to me or seeing glass sticking out of a pregnant stomach.

When I woke up the next day, the morning air was fresh and I felt like all my worries were behind me. When I finished my shower, Mama had cooked eggs, bacon, pancakes and hash browns. I was full, lookin' good and ready to see my baby, only he wasn't home. Theresa and Tasha weren't home either. Tasha was most likely at the hospital with Kim and no doubt Theresa's fast behind was with her boyfriend already. I probably needed some 'me' time anyway. Just then the doorbell rang and my 'me' time was over before it began.

Peeking out of the blinds, I wished I would've stayed in my room. Reggie's braids screamed for help and he was wearing the same dingy Rams jersey I'd seen him in two days earlier. I wanted to leave him out on the porch but I figured I should formally break up with him before he ended up seeing me with Aaron somewhere.

"Hey, I missed you," he beamed when I opened the door. He had the nerve to step towards me with his arms open for a hug. I started coughing from inhaling at least two days worth of weed off his jersey. From the look on his face, he could tell something was wrong. He claimed he missed me. He would never realize how much he'd missed in the past couple of days.

"We need to talk," was all I said as I pulled him off the porch and down the street to the park. We were both quiet for the short block until we were seated on a bench.

"What's wrong, baby?" He actually looked concerned and I had to wonder why I felt bad. I had no idea how we lasted almost a year anyway. I saw him maybe twice a week when he felt like being polite, we never went anywhere, never did anything, and we'd had sex every other month. He probably had a couple other girlfriends, though it was hard to think anyone else would put up with him.

"This isn't working out." I put it bluntly. He was stunned. I mean, he was downright *floored*! His face was a mixture of hurt, confusion, anger and pure hatred. I was hit with a quick pang of fear but it subsided. Reggie wouldn't put his hands on me. He couldn't be that crazy.

"It's that nigga, Aaron ain't it?" His leg was shaking and he began pumping his fist.

"Nobody is talkin' about Aaron right now. My life took a whole new turn the other day and you were nowhere to be found. When I needed some support, you weren't there for me." I hadn't realized until I felt my heartbeat that I was actually hurt. I was raising my voice and I was pissed at him for not caring what went on in my day to day life.

"So *you* are breakin' up wit' *me*?" He emphasized 'you' and 'me' as if *I* were the one who wasn't good enough for him; as if *I* were the one who didn't pay attention to him. As if *I* were the one who walked around not giving a damn how I carried myself. "I know it's that nigga! How long you been fuckin' him?"

"What?" I acted insulted. "I told you this has nothing to do with Aaron and I ain't been havin' sex with him!" I screamed back.

"So you ain't just gone break up wit me, you gone *lie* while you do it. You- stupid- hoe." Then his hands flew up to my neck. I closed my eyes and felt carpet beneath my feet. I knew if I could just get the knife up then it would be all over and my father would never be able to hurt me again. I pounded the knife in his chest again and again, each time my arms getting weaker from lack of oxygen. *Why the hell can't I slow him down? I can't let him win.* But as soon as the thought came, I was flung to the floor.

"You ain't worth it." I opened my eyes and Reggie was walking away, hands stuffed in his pockets. My butt suddenly hurt from hitting the ground instead of the plush white carpet I was expecting. Looking down at my hands, I realized I didn't even have a knife. If I had, would Reggie be laying on the ground next to me?

I bolted back up the street letting the summer breeze dry my tears. I was losing my mind. That was the only logical explanation. Aaron had said it was normal to hallucinate because I was obviously feeling guilty. Trying to kill my father all over again did not constitute guilt.

My room didn't provide the solace I needed. The dark cherry wood was too big for my small space and the pale mauve walls were closing in on me. The bed was too soft and I was sinking like I was in a Freddy Krueger movie. I jumped up for the phone but Aaron's mother informed me that he still wasn't home. Where the hell was he? I needed someone to talk to. I couldn't confess to my mother and it wasn't the best time to confide in my friends about my problems. My mind was ripping in two and I began to realize I was just as scared in my room as I was outside. Fishing the card out of my purse, I contemplated actually calling the therapist. I wondered guiltily, for a split second, if she was white and decided against the call. I tore the card into pieces and threw it away once and for all because in order for her to help me, she'd have to know the truth. That included admitting that Aaron and I had lied to the police. That included admitting that the man was asleep when I did what I did. That included having to go over every little detail of disgust I could remember. I would have to embarrass myself for someone I didn't know and try to justify why I let that crap go on for so long. No, I'd rather just talk to Aaron... if I could ever find him.

My body was drained and I figured a nap would suffice. Consciousness slipped away slowly. I levitated briefly, feeling like I was in Heaven. Then I began tumbling, slamming violently into jagged rocks in a dark tunnel. Blood seeped out from open gashes and my stomach rose up into my throat. The immense heat ripped at my clothes and blood seared my bare skin. Ironically, flames danced a halo around my head before engulfing my face.

"*You- killed- me…*"

My eyes shot open in pain. My hair was matted to my pillow with sweat. The clock read 6:45 p.m. I'd been out for five hours. I checked quickly to make sure my arms and legs were okay. Between deep, terrified breaths, I realized that I'd been to hell and back.

SIX

The corner of Grand and Osage was unusually busy and I found myself a little intimidated. The girls donned their short skirts and halter tops. The guys, a couple who were obviously selling, wore wife beaters and ridiculously baggy shorts. Any other day I would've smiled and waved as I walked past. That day I just wanted to get to the gas station, get my Strawberry Vess and Red Hot Ripplets, and get back home. I was still too shaken up from my dream.

The line was short and soon I was back out in the hot sun. I was used to the busy street and immune to the honking horns, but when I heard my name I quickened my step, hoping I wouldn't conjure up my father right there on the main street. I heard my name again and almost dropped my bag when a car swooped onto the street on front of me. When I saw who it was, my heart rate returned to normal, but then I was frustrated.

"You like my new ride?" My ex boyfriend, Chris, hung out the window but I kept walking. Seeing him was absolutely the very *last* thing I needed. Damn if he wasn't fine though. But that didn't matter. All that mattered was that a year ago I caught him at the park with his hands up some girl's shirt. And no matter how much he tried to deny it, I knew he was selling drugs. No way was a seventeen year old with no job ballin' that hard. "Aww, come on baby, don't do me like that." I walked teasingly up my porch steps, switching on purpose. The only thing that made him stop was that he never got any from me. He saw me in my little shorts and tight shirt and thought he missed me. His dick was the one talkin', not him, so I don't know why I stopped.

"What is it Chris?"

"I can't talk to you for a minute?" He was getting out of the car.

"About what, Chris?"

"Damn baby, it's like that?" He was on the steps.

"It's *like* that."

"What did I do?" He grinned in my face and I became instantly annoyed.

"I haven't heard from you in almost a year. Are you trying to impress me with your car or something?"

"Naw, I just saw you walking and thought I'd say 'hey'."

"Well, hey." I know I sounded real dry but I guess he wasn't trying to hear it.

"Wanna go for a ride?"

"Boy please. You musta lost it."

"Come on, just take a look at it." Grabbing my hand, he pulled me down the steps. I can't lie, his car was beautiful. The Monte Carlo had to be an '89. It was painted candy red with a white rag top and 24" rims. The windows wore a dark tint and the handles were chrome. I tried so hard not to look impressed but he'd really come up from the Camry he had when we were together. I opened the door and was overpowered by the new car smell. The interior was damn near sexy. Red stitching accented the snow white, leather seat and I guess he was done denying how he made his money. The word 'Candyman' was etched in the headrests, also in red stitching. The digital display in the wood grain set the whole thing off. I didn't have time to admire anything else because that bastard pushed me in and slammed the door. I attempted to get out but couldn't. The damn SS had child locks! Chris jumped in on the other side and he must've locked the windows too because I couldn't roll mine down.

"Chris, what the hell…"

"I missed you, Kyra." The nigga's eyes were glossy like he was actually about to cry. I just looked at him like he was crazy. When he started the car and pulled off, I was more pissed than afraid.

"Turn this car around, Chris." I tried to sound as calm as possible. I figured if I yelled and cursed he definitely wouldn't stop.

"I never stopped lovin' you Kyra."

"*Love*! We were together four months!"

"And you made me wait. Nobody ever held out on me before."

"Is that what this is about? You not gettin' any from me?"

"I think about you every day and how much I love you." He reached out to me and I shrank to the door.

"Chris, turn this car around!" I was wondering if he had popped a pill or something because he hadn't acted like that on my porch.

"No matter who I'm with I think about you, the one that got away." I checked the door and window again before trying to reach over him to deactivate the locks. He backhanded me. My cheek stung and fear shot through me like lightning.

"You can't leave me again!" What was going through his head and why the hell did I have to look in his car?

We were on the highway. I didn't even know which one. I'd been paying so much attention to Chris and how I was gonna get out of the car. He swooped onto an exit ramp that I didn't recognize. It was 8:25 and getting dark out. Chris pulled into an alley behind a vacant house and terror seized me.

"I want you." He tugged at my shorts and I screamed for help knowing no one would hear me.

"Please don't do this…" I begged, wishing I'd had sex with him when we were together. If I had, maybe I wouldn't have ended up in that situation.

"Don't fight me Kyra." He pulled so hard he ripped my shirt. Tears began to flow freely.

"See, that's how I know you still love me."

"Because I'm crying? Chris, you don't have to do this, please just take me home." He wasn't paying much attention to my begging, and my tears seemed to be exciting him. I fought like hell trying to keep him off me. I even tried punching at the windows, but when I turned from him he reached around and grabbed my breasts with both hands. Using his leverage, he yanked me backwards towards him. My back hit the gear shift and pain shot through my entire body.

"You gon' be mines tonight," he said as he slid the seats back. He gripped both my wrists with one hand while trying to unbutton my shorts. I wriggled around but it was no use. He forced his hands inside me. They were big and dry and I tried to stifle my screams because he seemed to get off on my pain. That, too, was no use. I couldn't conceal my agony as he scratched at my insides. He let go only to unbutton his pants. I took the opportunity to try and zip my shorts, but before I could get it done he was pushing me back in the reclined seat.

"I wanna feel yo' lips." *WHAT!! His ass had gone crazy!* The front seat was back so far that Chris was able to pin my arms on the back seat. I hadn't even realized he was naked from the waist down. Gotdamn horny Houdini! He began to straddle my face. I tried to lift my knee and catch him between the legs but I was too slow.

"Open those lips." I shook my head violently, surprisingly more afraid of that than the actual rape. "I said open your mouth." He took one of his knees and jammed it into my ear. Sharp pin pricks shot through my head. Like a machine, I opened my mouth obediently and let him slide in. As he moaned with pleasure, I took every ounce of wrath and disgust and bit down- hard. I was tempted to stop when he cried out in agony.

He let my arms go and began hitting me in the face.

"Let go you stupid bitch!" I figured if he could yell and hit, then he wasn't hurt enough. My head throbbed from his strong blows but I only bit down harder. His screams turned into incoherent, muffled whimpers and I gagged on blood. Satisfied, I loosened my grip and watched in triumph as he crumpled into the back seat. I unlocked the doors and let the night air bombard me as I ran in no particular direction. I was sore from Chris's massive fingers, but I ran anyway, powered by the vision of him crying and bleeding in his own back seat.

By the time I got to a bus stop I recognized, it was almost eleven. I took a seat in the very back, pulling my shirt together as much as I could. There was one other person on the bus besides the bus driver and me. I couldn't control my sobbing and I didn't care. I thought guiltily about Aaron and what he had to be thinking, not hearing from me all day.

It only took me a couple of minutes to get to his house from the bus stop. Eager to see him, I crept through the gangway around the side of the house until I came to his window. The only light was the glow from the television. I could, however, make out two of my best friends, Aaron and Theresa, lounging intimately under the covers.

SEVEN

My heart was breaking. As soon as the pain set in good, it was replaced by sheer malice. A single brick caught my eye and I smashed it against the window. I'd forgotten all about his parents and was sure I'd woken them up. Aaron had jumped up revealing his boxers and nude chest. Theresa yanked the covers up to her chin but not before I saw her bare breasts. I didn't give them time to get to the window before shooting out of the gangway. Hearing Aaron yelling my name made the tears flow like they had on the bus. I'd known Theresa since I was six and I'd confided in Aaron like I'd never confided in anyone in my life. I guess they just said fuck my feelings and did what the hell they wanted to do.

My shirt was flying open exposing my bra but I didn't care. Nothing really mattered at that moment. Not even how, when or why they got together. They were *together*. They were in bed, *together*, while Chris was trying to rape me. I turned, half hoping to see Aaron running after me. He wasn't. All three of them could kiss my ass.

I wished silently that Mama would be asleep when I got home. My wish came true and I crept up the stairs trying my best to hold in my exhausted cries. Throwing myself on the bed, I had to think back on the past couple of days. What fifteen year old has to deal with all that drama? The sight of Theresa and Aaron half naked together kept running through my mind and I really didn't sleep well.

By the time I did wake up, there were five calls on the caller I.D. from Aaron's house. No calls from Theresa though. I wondered if she'd had the nerve to spend the night at Aaron's and call from there or if she went home and didn't bother calling at all. I convinced myself that I didn't care, even though I stayed in the tub for an hour wondering what the hell I was going to say or do when one of them finally caught up with me.

After I got dressed, Mama peeked in to tell me that Aaron and Tasha had each called twice. No Theresa. I figured she either didn't care or was simply too ashamed, so I tried to block her from my mind while I called Tasha. She answered on the first ring.

"Hey Tasha," I felt relieved just to hear her voice. I wondered if she'd heard from Theresa.

"Hey." She wasn't her normal upbeat self.

"How's Kim?" Hearing Tasha's voice, I was scared to ask but I did anyway.

"Not good." My shoulders sagged and I wanted her to stop but I didn't interrupt. "They didn't get all the glass out and now there's an infection." Everything in the room was spinning.

"So what does that mean? They can remove it can't they." There was silence on the other end before I heard her soft sobs. "I'm on my way."

Mama drove like a crazy woman when I told her what was going on. We stopped to pick up Tasha who'd taken a break from the hospital. We met her parents in the chapel where we prayed, talked, laughed and cried until we were overhead paged to her room. Mama and I huddled together while the doctor told the immediate family that Kim had a 20% chance of survival but they were keeping the baby healthy. Three days later, Kim was still fighting and her chances went up to 50%. The baby was getting stronger but Tasha, on the other hand, wasn't.

I'd spent the past three days between home, the hospital, and Tasha's house. I really thought that the better Kim got, the better Tasha would get, but it didn't work out that way. Mama had the family over for dinner and we both tried to be positive forces in their lives even though we were suffering ourselves. On top of worrying about Kim, Mama was still trying to keep up the nonchalant façade over losing my father. I personally felt like Chicken Little trying to run away from pieces of falling sky. Everywhere I turned life seemed to be letting me down. I hadn't had any more dreams about my father, but that was probably because I'd been dreaming about Aaron and Theresa every night. It was becoming impossible for me to avoid Aaron's constant calls, but Theresa had become a pro at avoiding me, magically calling or visiting Tasha only when I wasn't around.

Kim had fought her way back to health and had been in the hospital a little over a week when I ran into Theresa at Tasha's house. It had been five days since I caught her and Aaron. Tasha's mother let me in and said Tasha was upstairs in the tub, but said nothing about Theresa. I was unpleasantly surprised. She was seated in a chair by the window and jumped when I walked in. Tension filled the air for the next few minutes while I waited for Theresa to say something… anything.

"What you saw the other night, it wasn't what it looked like." Bad move. She started off with a lie. "Me and Aaron are *just friends*." I wanted to punch her in her face. I thought back to what I saw, both of them, topless, under the covers. She hadn't even bothered to *call* me.

"Whatever you say, Theresa." I tried my best to bite my tongue and stay calm. I wasn't there to fight her, I was there for Tasha.

"Don't be like that."

"Don't be like what?" I snapped back. "You expect me to be cool after finding you and *my* man naked together? *And* you been ignoring me." Plus, Reggie had tried to strangle me in the park in broad daylight and I damn near had to bite off Chris' dick to keep him from raping me. But hey, my problems were my own right?

"I told you it wasn't what it looked like."

"So ya'll weren't naked together?" I was hot. My head started throbbing and I fought back tears.

"Yes, but…"

"Ya'll didn't have sex?"

"Yeah, but…"

"Yeah but what?" I was practically screaming. I woulda been a fool to think that they hadn't slept together, but hearing her admit it so matter-of-factly, it was a slap in the face. "I guess now you're gonna tell me it was an accident, that ya'll didn't mean to do it." I was standing up now, still trying to control my temper.

"It *was* an accident, Kyra, I swear." Theresa's tears looked like the ones I squeezed out for the police after I'd murdered my father.

"What the hell were you even doing over there for the accident to happen? How do you even know where he stays?"

"Kyra *he* was trying to holla at *me*…"

"And you couldn't have told me that? Long as I've liked him and you couldn't say anything to me about him wantin' you?"

"I wanted to, I did but…" I threw my hand in the air, cutting her off. I wanted to know why and for how long, but then again, I didn't want to know. In the end, they still did what they did and I still felt like shit. We sat there, quiet, until I realized that we'd been really loud and Tasha was still in her bathroom. At first I knocked softly. After a couple of minutes, Theresa and I were pounding on the door and calling her name. Her parents weren't far behind us and her father was able to kick open the door. The sight floored me. Tasha was in a tub of blood, unconscious and breathing shallowly.

The ride to the emergency room was a blur. Time stood still as I waited to hear the fate of yet another friend. Tasha had

35

slit her wrists but, according to the doctor, had actually saved her own life when she put her arms in the tub instead of hanging them over the side. The doctor informed us that, physically, Tasha would be fine. How she was doing mentally was a different story. Kim and the baby had been doing a lot better so we were all confused as to what was going on in Tasha's head. I thought about the things that had happened to me over the past few years and almost understood her reasoning. As close as we all thought we were, the past week proved that we had no idea what was really going on in each others' minds.

EIGHT

I missed my period. I'd heard that extreme stress can throw you off and after the first week I was late, I believed that was my problem. Two weeks after I was supposed to start, I panicked. It just couldn't be possible. I didn't feel like spending money on a test and hiding in my own bathroom to take it. So I lied to my mama and rode the bus to the Planned Parenthood up the street.

I was nervous as hell sitting in that waiting room. I really didn't feel like filling out their questionnaire either. I just wanted to take my free test, find out it was negative, and go home. *First day of last menstrual period: June 15th*. It was July 29th, way over the usual twenty-eight days later. *Number of sexual partners: None of your damn business*. Why did they need to know that anyway? Did I miss something or doesn't it only take one partner to get pregnant? I erased my answer and left it blank.

I'd been in the waiting room for twenty minutes after I peed in the cup. "Girl if I'm pregnant I'll have to get an abortion," one of the girls in the room told her friend.

"If I'm pregnant, this'll be my third abortion. Don't worry, they get easier," the friend replied.

"Kyra Blasik." I was glad the nurse called my name because I didn't feel like listening to those stupid females. "So how are you doing today?" The nurse was chunky and dark-skinned. Her dimples sat deep in her pretty face.

"Alright." I settled in the hard seat across the table from her.

"Have you been feeling any differently?" She smiled and I was getting irritated. Why couldn't I just get my answer and go?

"No, I haven't." She opened a small folder and looked over it. I felt a headache coming on because for the first time in my life, I actually believed I could be pregnant. Would I be like the girls in the waiting room? What would I tell my mama? I was trippin'. All I needed from that woman was to find out why I wasn't bleeding because I certainly was NOT pregnant.

"It says here that you are approximately four weeks pregnant." She was lying. She had to be. But when she handed me the result sheet there it was big as day: POSITIVE.

"Do you need a few minutes?" She could see the distress in my face. She seemed to be sympathetic even though, to her, I was probably just another young girl in trouble.

"No, thank you." I told her. I needed fresh air. I needed to throw up. I needed to get out of that room, away from that nurse. My head was throbbing. I'd cried so much over Tasha, Aaron and Theresa that I didn't have tears left for myself. I stood outside the building with my mind completely blank for fifteen minutes. Two busses passed me before I decided to walk home. Then a thought hit me. A month ago I was with Reggie... and Aaron... and my father was alive. So which one was it?

The bus had only taken five minutes to get to Planned Parenthood but it took me half an hour to walk back home. Normally, walking down Grand Blvd., I would've been hungry. But between Taco Bell, KFC, White Castle and Pizza Hut, I just felt sick. I knew my mind wasn't playing tricks on me. What I was feeling wasn't the infamous morning sickness. I was sick to death from the idea that I was carrying someone's child. No matter whose it was, I didn't want it. Reggie was nasty and abusive, Aaron was a cheating bastard who I hadn't seen or heard from in forever, and my father was the worse man I'd ever met. I had no choice. I had to get rid of the baby.

When I finally got home, Aaron had the nerve to be on my front porch. I hadn't seen him since that dreadful night over three weeks ago and eventually, after I never answered his calls, they'd stopped. I fought to keep my cool. What were the odds that he'd shown up *that* day, and was waiting for me when I got home from Planned Parenthood. I wanted to beat his ass and fall into his arms all at the same time. I was confused because seeing him still made my heart jump. I wanted to hug him and tell him I was pregnant. Tell him about Chris and how he'd hurt me. Tell him about Reggie flipping out. Cry out to him about Tasha. Question him about Theresa… but I wouldn't let my guard down so easily.

"Hey Kyra," he said after we'd locked eyes for a moment. He put his arms out and I couldn't stop myself. I didn't hug hard though. "I missed you." I could've broke down and cried right there if I hadn't been tired of crying.

"I missed you too," I told him. I couldn't stand being a punk so I pulled away.

"How have you been?"

"Why do you care?" I tried to act pissed but I was happy he'd come to see me.

"I swear I never meant to hurt you."

"So what were you trying to do, Aaron?" By this time we'd sat on opposite sides of the porch and were facing each other.

"It was fucked up, I know. But I been trying to apologize forever."

"What will apologizing do? Especially after what I been through. And you do me like *that*. Both of ya'll." I was glad I was able to block the images from my mind. "I wanna know what happened." He looked at me at first like he wasn't going to say anything. In that case, I would've sent him home.

"I'm always running into her or Tasha at the corner store," he started off. "A couple days after that stuff with your pops, I ran into Theresa. She was saying how crazy everything was with you and Kim and we were just walking and talking and ended up at my house." I squirmed a little, afraid to hear the rest. It would probably only be half the truth anyway. "She started talking about the first day I saw ya'll on your porch and joked about her being outside instead of you when I came back. I laughed but I was wondering what she was getting at." There was a timid look in his eye and I wanted so badly to tell him it was okay and that I would forgive him if he promised not to do it again. But I knew I could never forgive either of them, no matter how much I loved them.

"I don't even remember what all we talked about but I ended up letting her in. I don't even know why because I swear I wasn't thinking about doing anything with her."

"One of my best friends was flirtin' with you so you decided to let her in and expect me to be stupid enough to believe you weren't thinkin' about having sex wit' her! Or were *you* stupid enough to think she wasn't tryin' to get wit' you?" He looked surprised, like I wasn't supposed to interrupt him.

"Kyra, it wasn't even like that. I wasn't thinking about sex and I'm sure Theresa wasn't either."

"Oh I'm sorry." I put my hand on my chest like I was hurt by my own mistake. "I should've realized ya'll couldn't have been thinkin' about sex when you went back to your bedroom. Definitely not thinkin' about sex when ya'll was takin' off clothes! I know my friend is a freak but she probably wasn't thinkin' about sex when she was suckin' yo' dick!" By this time I was almost in his face. "And damn if I wasn't losing my mind expecting' ya'll to be thinking about sex while you were fuckin'!" He was not amused by my sarcasm. I wanted to push him over the side of the porch. He cheated on me with my best friend and had the nerve to look at me like *he* was pissed.

My adrenaline was pumping and I wanted to fight him so bad. I wished I would've let Theresa talk that day at Tasha's house so I'd have both of their sorry ass stories to compare.

"Kyra- I told you- it wasn't- like that."

"Aaron- tell me then- what- was it like?" I used the same dramatic pauses he did and he rolled his eyes like a female.

"I don't see the humor in this, Kyra."

"I don't either, Aaron. But I did enough crying the day I had to see ya'll all comfy cozy in yo' bed. I had enough nightmares about ya'll havin' sex over and over again. And I got too much goin' on in my life right now so excuse me if I don't have the time or energy to drop another tear for *you*." I'd hurt his feelings. He looked like he was on the verge of tears and I wanted so bad to see him break down. I think I *needed* to see it. I needed to know his heart was breaking just like mine had.

"I'm sorry, Kyra. I know it's not enough but I just been missin' you and thinkin' about you and I wanted to apologize. If you can ever find it in your heart to talk to me again, just call me please." I stood still, holding in the hurt, and let him kiss my cheek. He turned to look back at me once more before disappearing down the alley. I crumpled onto the porch and watched my tears as they finally fell and scared the ants away.

Mama was watching *The Color Purple* and I could smell meatloaf in the oven when I walked in. I thought about watching it with her but instead, I just let her know I was home. She stopped me to tell me I'd just missed Aaron. I said okay and went up to my room where I cranked up my Whitney Houston C.D. and belted out the words as loud and heartfelt as I could:

All at once, I'm drifting on a lonely sea,
Wishing you'd come back to me.
And that's all that matters now.
All at once...

NINE

M_y legs gapped open wider as I screamed uncontrollably. Sweat poured down my face and my thighs burned. I experienced feelings I never felt before and all of a sudden I was aware of everyone who was watching and immediately wanted them out. Epidural my ass. I felt every contraction, every ache, and every pain, even with that tube pumping anesthesia into my back. And after seventeen hours of labor, I didn't even know if I still wanted the damn baby.

"He's coming!" The Doogie Howser look-alike seemed more excited than Mama and Tasha who'd resorted to praying in a corner. The pain had become so overwhelming that I just wanted to pass out. I wondered whose eyes my son would have, Aaron's, Reggie's, mine and my mama's, or, God forbid, my father's.

"One more big push, Kyra!" Doogie Howser needed to shut the hell up! I wanted to switch places with him for just a minute. Let him feel my pain and see how excited he'd be then. "Almost, almost..." I closed my eyes and screamed bloody murder as the excruciating pain of my insides being ripped out shot through the length of my body. It happened so quick that I thought I would go into shock. When I opened my eyes, instead of a child, there stood my father, covered in blood like he'd been rejuvenated. The stain on his shirt paled in comparison to what I was seeing. He was Carrie and the hospital room was a scene from Amityville Horror. Mama screamed and Tasha passed out. Dr. Doogie Howser shrank over to a far corner. His feet kept

pushing back like he was trying to go straight through the wall into the hallway. The throbbing agony of the gaping hole my father had left between my legs began to seep through the devastation. My vision became blurry as my father burst into maniacal laughter. I dropped my head back onto the pillow and my eyes slowly closed, but not before I heard those infamous words...
"*You- killed- me...*"

***

I went out onto the porch in my sleeping shorts and t-shirt. There was a nice, early morning breeze helping to soothe away the crazy nightmare. As I settled on the ledge, a gust of wind blew paper onto the porch. It was a *Whirl* newspaper, famous for printing gossip of who stole from who, who shot who and who got locked up for domestic violence or selling drugs. I was about to kick it down when I caught a familiar face. Chris sneered up at me with a headline that read: *Young Man Slain in Drug Deal Gone Bad.*

My feelings were mixed as I slowly picked up the paper and began to read. Confusion set in, followed by fear. Chris had not been the one killed in the drug deal. According to an unnamed 'friend', Chris was shorted on a deal. Apparently, he shot the guy in the face five times and took the money and drugs. He'd been caught and arrested, but the thought of what could've happened in the alley that night lingered in the back of my mind. I ended up crumpling the paper and throwing it in the dumpster.

It was early and I didn't know if Planned Parenthood was open but I called anyway and a pleasant sounding woman answered the phone.

"Yes, I'm calling to see how late in the pregnancy an abortion can be performed."

"We perform abortions up until the second trimester begins."

"And how much are they?"

"Three fifty, without insurance."

"Thank you." I knew I couldn't use insurance because Mama would find out. So I had two months to come up with Three hundred fifty dollars. I spread out on my bed making a mental list of who I knew and how they could or couldn't help me. I could never tell Mama. I could only imagine the reaction to her fifteen year old daughter being pregnant and not knowing who the father was. I wouldn't dare ask anyone in my family. They were so nosy and talked so much that, even if I did lie, something would get back to my mama and she'd want to know what I needed the money for. I knew Tasha's parents had the money. Kim was still in the hospital and close to 80% and I'd talked to Tasha who was recovering well under her parent's supervision. She still wasn't ready to discuss her underlying issues and I really didn't wanna bother their parents with my problems too. I vowed not to tell Aaron I was pregnant, that there was a 33% chance it could be his, and then ask him to help me get rid of it. I hadn't heard from Theresa so she could kiss my ass. Of course asking Reggie was out of the question. The list was short and sad, making me realize I was on my own.

I was still six months away from my 16th birthday so couldn't work. I thought about a yard sale but I couldn't think of anything I could sell. Nothing adding up to three hundred fifty dollars. The thought of a suga daddy briefly crossed my mind. Lots of older men liked paying to spend time with pretty ladies. I'd have to meet some strange man and con him into trusting me enough to give up his money. I only had two months though. Was I that persuasive? Was I that trifling?

I ran out of ideas and thought I'd take a shower to ease my mind. When I finished, I stood in front of my full length mirror admiring myself. I was petite with a caramel complexion, a small waist, thick thighs, and perfect 34 Ds. I turned to the side, sucking in my already flat stomach and tracing my round behind with my hands. Damn, I could model for Playboy.

Domino's *Sweet Potato Pie* played in my head and I danced around a bit before another idea hit me. I could strip! I heard the money was fast and easy so I could most likely get what I needed in a couple of days and quit. I pulled my micros back off my face and thought that, with a little make-up, I could pass for eighteen, maybe twenty. I was scared as hell going through my closet. What do you wear to a stripper interview?

After two hours of questioning and second guessing myself, Mama told me she was going to the grocery store. I took that as a sign to go through her clothes and makeup. By the time I finished, I had on black miniskirt and a red bra under a black lace top. I'd stolen a pair of black stilettos out of Mama's closet and tied them up to my knees. My finger and toe-nails had been painted a bright red and I'd pulled my braids up. I didn't want to look that much like a hooker so I only put on eye and lip liner, mascara and lip gloss. I thought I was looking good until I stepped out on the porch and thought about other people seeing me. I started feeling self conscious and almost went back in the house. Then I thought about my nightmare and made my way to the bus stop.

I made sure I folded my arms to hide my bra when I got on the bus. Two busses and forty minutes later, I got off I was at my destination. I got off at the stop almost three blocks from the club because I didn't want people to see me get off right in front of it. I'd heard about Top Heavy from one of Kim's old boyfriends. I prayed he wasn't a regular. Then again, he may not have recognize me anyway. Walking slowly towards the club, I began to second guess myself again. The whole situation was crazy. What the hell was I thinking? "I work at Top Heavy," I said aloud. It didn't even sound right coming out of my mouth. A car was coming so I ducked into an alley. If I was that ashamed of someone seeing me walking *towards* the club, then how was I supposed to dance *in* it?

I kept down the alley almost laughing to myself. Just

because I had a nice body and could dance did not mean I had what it took to work at a strip club. I was almost ready to take Mama's stilettos off as I hobbled clumsily through the loose gravel. A car pulled in behind me but I didn't care until I heard it slowing down. The driver stopped beside me grinning hard and showing his shiny grill.

"How much babe?" I looked up from my shoe with disgust. He actually thought I was a hooker! I *was* bent over in a tight skirt in the middle of an alley. "You hear me, Boo? Can I get that?" I stood up straight and put my hands on my hips wishing I had a stick of gum to smack on like the hookers on *Law and Order*. I couldn't believe what I was doing.

"What'chu got?" Underneath my flirtatious smile I wondered if I could actually turn into a hoe to get rid of a baby.

"I got five hundred dollars for you, just get in. *Please*. You won't regret it. I promise, baby." He sounded desperate and way too anxious. What if he was a cop? What if he was married? What if he was crazy and wanted me to do something ignorant in his back seat?

"Sorry sweetie. Not today." I tried to walk away but, of course, he eased along with me.

"Not even for this?" I glanced over at his fan of bills, rolled my eyes, and forced myself to keep walking. "Be that way then, bitch. It was probably only worth ten dollars anyway." He zoomed off down the alley. I started to get pissed but decided to be relieved he'd pulled off in the first place. During the bus ride home, there were so many thoughts filling my head. After it seemed I'd exhausted all the possibilities, I couldn't believe I was going to kill a baby anyway. *My* baby. I started trying to convince myself that I wouldn't need Reggie or Aaron; that eventually Mama's disappointment would wear off; that a baby at sixteen would not ruin my life. I was halfway convinced by the time I got off the bus.

Mama was putting up groceries and I yelled 'hi' while

running up the steps to change. The last thing I needed was her to see me like that. When I got back downstairs, seasoned steaks were marinating on the counter and Mama was peeling potatoes. I sat at the table next to her and began helping.

"Mama," I inhaled deeply then let a slow, nervous breath escape before going on. "We need to talk."

PART TWO

if it ain't one thing, it's another

TEN

JaLea Michelle was born on March 31, 1991. She was beautiful. Chunky and chocolate with huge hazel eyes and curls of jet black hair. Mama was asleep in the corner and Kim and Tasha had just left with Kim's seven month old, Isaiah. All the commotion had died down and I was breastfeeding my daughter. It hurt like hell but I wouldn't have traded that moment for anything. A knock at the door broke my concentration.

"Come in." I was irritated with whoever had the nerve to interrupt my private time until Aaron stepped in with balloons and roses. He stood over me in quiet astonishment until I was done feeding JaLea. I handed her over and he took her gently. I watched as he bounced around lightly, looking into her eyes. He was staring at his twin. Watching them was Heaven.

It had taken Mama a while to calm down after I told her I was pregnant, but when she did, she talked me into calling Aaron. Even after I told Mama about Aaron and Theresa, she convinced me that that didn't change the fact that he may be the father. It took me a couple weeks to conjure up the nerve to call him. It took another two weeks to build up enough courage to tell him I may be pregnant with his child. He was scared, but happy. I didn't want him to get his hopes up but he did anyway. He began showering me with attention, catering to my every silly, pregnant need. He was at the hospital at 6 a.m., forty-five minutes after I got there, and waited patiently until Kim and Tasha had left. He was seeing his daughter for the first time.

"I don't wanna take the test," he said, not taking his eyes off JaLea. We'd agreed to have a paternity test, but after seeing that little girl's face, we were both convinced.

"I don't either," I agreed. Aaron's eyes welled up with tears and it was at that moment I decided to give her his last name, Washington, instead of mine.

Aaron and I spent the next two days spoiling JaLea rotten before we even left the hospital. Every visitor we had said she looked just like Aaron, and I thanked God for both of them. That little girl meant more to me than anything else in the world. Holding her made me forget about the year before, and Aaron and I were on very good terms even though we hadn't gotten back together.

The last day of our stay, Mama and Aaron were helping me get all of JaLea's things together. There was a soft knock on the door and Aaron, thinking it was the nurse with discharge papers, said to come in. The three of us froze as Theresa walked in. After I'd decided to try and mend fences with her and Aaron, there was still space between us. Aaron was happy to be back in my life but Theresa seemed distant. I hadn't talked to her in two months. It had been longer since I'd seen her.

"Hey, thought I missed you." She came closer and I saw the baby bump in her stomach. Theresa was pregnant and hadn't said a word. If she had told Tasha, Tasha had kept it to herself. "How are you doing?" She smiled at Mama and I guess she was ignoring Aaron because she walked past him right to me and JaLea. "I'm really happy for you. She's adorable."

"Thank you." She seemed to truly mean it. I wanted to congratulate her on her pregnancy but she obviously hadn't wanted me to know she was pregnant, so I kept my mouth shut. Then she turned and left without another word. We just looked around at each other and kept packing. I wasn't about to let

Theresa upset me.

Little did I know that Kim, Tasha and their parents had been busy turning my room into a nursery. They didn't touch the mauve walls but they'd refinished the crib and dresser I had, making it match my dark cherry wood. They'd taken out the T.V. stand and put the television on top of the dresser to make room for JaLea's corner and my new rocking chair. She already had clothes, but they'd filled all five of her little drawers with more, and there was a small stand next to my bed packed with bottles, wash cloths, socks and bibs. I looked over at Aaron who was just as amazed as I was.

"Look under the bed," Tasha told Aaron. He put JaLea down and stooped. I watched him pull out bag after bag after bag of pampers and I was outdone. After hugs, kisses and many thank you's, we were left alone with our daughter. I would've loved to just be able to enjoy watching Aaron talk to JaLea, but, being the type of female I was, I had to mess it up.

"So is it yours?"

"What?" He didn't look up.

"Theresa's baby." He stopped rocking.

"I thought we put all that behind us Kyra. I ain't talked to Theresa in months."

"How many *months*?"

"It's *not* my baby." He looked me dead in my eyes and didn't blink, so I believed him. Besides, he'd been in my face and at my house so much while I was pregnant. He hadn't had time for anyone else... hopefully.

It took a full month for Tasha to talk me into leaving JaLea with Aaron and taking a ride with her in her new car.

"So I hear we're gonna be sharing a tutor," she said once I got in the car. We'd both missed a lot of school. I had been just plain lazy while I was pregnant and Tasha had been recovering. The principle threatened to hold us back so our parents found a tutor. Five hours a day and I was done by the time Aaron got of school. I nodded at her, admiring the car.

"Why didn't you tell me Theresa was pregnant?" I asked.

"Theresa's pregnant!" Tasha almost drove through her stop sign.

"Don't tell me you didn't know."

"I swear, I didn't." I glared at her and she laughed. "I talk to her every blue moon and she never, *ever* told me she was pregnant. I told her she needed to talk to you or come see you or something but she didn't tell me anything about being pregnant. And she stopped coming to see me a long time ago." She looked at me and shook her head, still laughing.

"What is so funny?"

"You need to quit," she told me.

"Quit what?"

"I know what you're thinking, and I really don't think Aaron would be that dumb."

"He was dumb once, he can be dumb twice."

"Come off of it Kyra. That boy loves the hell outta you, believe me." The air was quiet between us.

"Do you know something I don't?"

"Nope." She answered too quickly.

"Talk to me, Tasha."

"I don't know anything." I stared her down until she cracked. "Okay Kyra, damn!" She took a deep breath and I braced myself for whatever was coming. "Theresa always wanted Aaron. Loved you like a sister, but couldn't stand the fact that Aaron wanted you. It always sounded so petty and I kept telling her to stop trippin. The south side is crawling with fine brothas. But after that day you came over to tell us about Aaron and your daddy, she was… different. I called her all upset about Kim and all she kept saying was 'I can't believe Aaron and Kyra had sex.' *I* couldn't believe her ass was being that selfish. When she finally got around to telling me about her and

Aaron, I'd already heard it from you. She felt bad that you caught them, but she was proud of herself because she called herself seducing him. According to her, she practically had to rape him." I knew Tasha wouldn't lie to me. She had no reason to. But I would rather have heard 'it was an accident.'

"But Tasha, when I got there they were sleep in his bed," I recalled painfully.

"Well, she said Aaron got pissed when she wouldn't leave and he went to sleep on her ass. Instead of leaving like he told her, this heffa takes her clothes back off and climbs back in the bed. And she got cursed out again after you ran off. She was happy anyway because she'd been wondering about the dick long as you had. She was jealous as hell." I sank back in the seat folding my arms.

"Some *friend*, huh?" I asked. I wasn't surprised. I wasn't even pissed at Tasha for not telling. I would've kept the secret too if I thought it was best for my friends. "So…" I chose my words carefully. "You got any more secrets?" She was quiet. I knew Tasha hadn't spoken a word of her attempted suicide to anyone. No one asked about it and, eventually, it was like it never happened at all. But I was nosy and Tasha was my best friend. She looked uneasy because she knew what I was hinting at. I thought about changing the subject but I couldn't think of anything else to say.

"I was pregnant." She said *was*. I almost hurt my neck jerking to look at her. "I couldn't tell anybody because I didn't want it." I subconsciously pictured Tasha at the Top Heavy club trying to make money and wondered how she was able to afford the abortion. "Remember the asshole I was talking to right after we found out Kim was pregnant?" I nodded. "You know I broke up with him because he gave me crabs with his nasty ass. Then a week later, I came home from school and Kim was on the porch cursing him out because he had the nerve to go over there to holla at *her*. Two weeks later I found out I was pregnant. I didn't have the money for an abortion so I had to get rid of it myself." I was confused until she pulled over, teary-eyed, to tell me the horrible story of torturing herself with pills and alcohol. I remembered her not being in school for a couple weeks. She claimed at the time she was just really sick. "It took a few days, but I did it. I miscarried in my bathroom and spent hours cleaning it up. No one ever knew."

I felt like shit. I wished I would've been there for her. Hell, I even wished Theresa would've been there so Tasha wouldn't have had to go through that by herself. I wanted to be upset that she'd kept something so big from me but I stayed quiet. I still wasn't planning on telling her about my father.

"When Kim had her accident, it all came rushing back to me so quick. I couldn't stand myself for what I did. Kim had an accident and almost lost her baby but I *killed* a *baby... my* baby. And I did it on purpose." I wondered what her hell must be like, watching Kim and I with our kids. Her eyes were still glossy but there were no tears on her cheeks, only disbelief in her voice. All I could do was hug her.

ELEVEN

I'd just finished feeding JaLea when Aaron walked in. I'd seen him every day for over two months and he never ceased to amaze me. He was still as sexy as the day I met him.

"How are my girls doing?" He kissed JaLea and took her for her burp.

"Good," I answered, trying my best not to stare at him. He wore khaki's, white Air Forces, and a black and white striped polo shirt. Nothing big, but he still turned me on. His gold cross dangled on his chain close to the baby's face and he smiled at her. Damn I loved that smile. I'd managed not to have sex since I found out I was pregnant. *Eleven months*! As sexy as Aaron was and as horny as I'd been, I was surprised I hadn't laid him out. We weren't back together but he *was* my baby's daddy, and that was the only excuse I needed to get some, right?

I watched Aaron lay JaLea down for her nap, turn on the television, and plop on the bed. My eyes moved from his braids to his full lips. I thought about how good it had felt to be in his arms and my eyes settled on the zipper of his jeans. I could feel the heartbeat between my legs getting stronger. It spread through my body making my nipples hard. He felt me staring and laughed.

"What?" I asked, trying my best to sound innocent.

"I see how you been lookin' at me," he said.

"And how have I been looking at you?"

"You miss me." He got up from the bed.

"You're over here *every* day! How could I miss you?"

"You miss this." He bent over the rocking chair and kissed me, sticking his tongue deep in my mouth. *DAMN*! I hadn't even had a *kiss* in eleven months. It's a shame when a kiss can almost make you cum. He backed up, looking me straight in the eyes, and I wanted to tackle him back onto the bed. "I missed you too, Kyra." I was still reeling from his kiss. "I swear to you. Nothing else went on between me and Theresa. What did happen was stupid and it meant nothing. I really want you to forgive me. I need you to." I wouldn't tell him about my conversation with Tasha. He could kiss up all he wanted. "You and JaLea mean everything to me."

"What are you getting at Aaron?"

"I wanna get back wit'chu. You know that." I did know that. And I wanted him just as much, if not more. "We need to stop playin' games." I rocked a little, making him frustrated, and he sat back on the bed. I wondered to myself what would change. He was already over everyday, we would never really go anywhere, but that was mostly because I never wanted to leave Jalea.

"So what's gonna be different, sex?"

"It's not even about sex! I wanna hold you and tell you I love you. I wanna be a family." Aaron told me he loved me. I wanted to melt but I kept my composure.

"Do you think we can go back to the way it used to be?"

"When? We never had a chance to be together. And I don't wanna just be friends. You don't know how it drives me crazy bein' over here everyday knowin' you won't accept me as anything other than JaLea's father. And you still think I'm messin' around."

I wanted to tell him I believed him and that I'd already forgiven him, but instead I just walked over and hugged him.

"I love you too," was all I could get out. And it was that easy. I thought to myself that I shouldn't have been so stubborn, but, at the same time, he had to learn a lesson. All that was left to do was make up.

We made up three times on a sweaty, passionate rollercoaster fueled by eleven months of sexual frustration. By the time JaLea woke up, we were worn out but decided to walk to the gas station to get some air.

Aaron had the baby in her carrier on his chest and we laughed and talked until we rounded the corner. Reggie was leaning against the wall beside the door. I knew Aaron wasn't thinking too much about him being there, but my chest started hurting thinking about my last run in with Reggie. Aaron knew nothing about it.

"What's up Kyra?" How did I know he'd be ignorant enough to speak to me when the last time I saw him he'd tried to choke me?

I didn't respond.

"What's up Reggie?" Aaron asked. Reggie pretended not to hear him and didn't take his eyes off me.

"I heard you got a lil' shorty. Congratulations."

"Thank you." Aaron answered again. This time Reggie looked annoyed because *I* wasn't the one answering his questions.

"Yeah, I got a lil' shorty on the way too." I didn't give a damn what was going on in his life. I just wanted to get in the store but, by this time, he was blocking the door.

"Congratulations." That time when Aaron answered, it was almost comical. I would've laughed if Theresa hadn't walked out of the store.

"Hey baby." Reggie kissed Theresa on the cheek and rubbed her belly. Aaron and I couldn't believe our eyes. Theresa looked like she'd seen a ghost.

"*Reggie* is your baby daddy!" I yelled at her. Her facial expression changed and she became defensive.

"You were *done* with him. You *played* him for Aaron."

"But I wasn't done with *Aaron* was I? You ain't got nothin' better to do so you run after niggas I already been with?!"

"Don't act like I'm desperate, Kyra."

"Oh you're not desperate? You can't find somebody to fuck on your own, you gotta go through me?"

"Looks like we got a couple things in common man," Reggie nudged Aaron playfully.

"Don't touch me." Aaron didn't find the situation amusing.

"Don't try to act all high and mighty now when you slept with both of them in the same day." Before I could even open my mouth, she crossed the line even further. "Oh damn, I forgot you slept with your daddy that day too!" Before I could stop myself, my fist flew forward, catching her nose and she stumbled. Aaron stopped my next punch and started pulling me away.

"I can't believe that bitch hit me." Theresa leaned onto Reggie for support.

"Believe it, hoe!" I screamed back.

"Kyra calm down." Aaron was pulling me faster. I hadn't noticed until that moment how many people were outside. I knew everyone had heard my business and they were all looking at me like I was nasty, wondering if it was true that I had slept with my father. No doubt they all felt bad for Theresa. Of course I was the bad person. After all, *I* was the one who punched a pregnant girl in the face. *I* was the one who was sleeping around; *I* was the one yelling like I was crazy.

"I know you heard what she said!" I yelled at Aaron.

"Yeah she was wrong. But I heard you going off on her for being with Reggie. Why would you even care?"

"I went off on her for being a hoe and going behind my back, not once, but twice. She was supposed to be my best friend. Friends are not supposed to share boyfriends and she had a lil' too much of what I had."

"Don't say it like that," Aaron sounded disgusted.

"How else can I say it? The four of us might as well have one big ass orgy!"

"Kyra, that's nasty."

"Why, because of Reggie? You already slept with Theresa so ain't nothin' new there."

"I'm not about to argue with you about this." So we didn't. He took JaLea upstairs while I stayed out on the porch thinking about Theresa. She'd slept with my baby's daddy, and my ex was her baby's daddy. What the hell was she thinking when she got with dirty, nasty Reggie, anyway? I knew I had told her plenty of stories about him. I couldn't even put my finger on why I was with him in the first place.

I felt self-centered for thinking it, but their relationship had to be about me. I thought back to what Tasha said about Theresa being jealous of me. Could she be jealous enough to hook up with *Reggie* though? What the hell was she trying to get back at me for?

TWELVE

 Close to the end of June, it rained for a week straight. Surprisingly, Mama had been letting Aaron spend the night since school let out. I suggested he just move in. She told me I was pushing it. I wondered if she figured we'd been having sex again… everyday, sometimes twice a day. I laughed thinking about the night before when Aaron tried to stick a pillow in my mouth to muffle my screams.

 "Staring won't make the rain go away." Mama came up beside me and sat down on the bay window bench. I could smell the Dove and baby powder on her and thought back to a time when I could lay in her lap. I stole a glance while she looked out the window. She was just a little darker than me and looked good to be pushing forty. Her shoulder length hair was feathered off her face. She kept her eye brows neat and arched and didn't even have to smile to show her dimples. Her waist was small and she didn't need a bra under her orange sundress. I secretly hoped I still looked that good when I turned thirty-seven.

 "Aaron and JaLea are sleep so I came downstairs."

 "So how are things going with the three of you?"

 "A lot better." I smiled thinking about how good Aaron had been with me and JaLea.

 "Look at that smile!" She grinned. "What about your friends? How are they?"

 "Tasha and Kim are fine." I'd been able to avoid Mama's questions about Theresa up until then.

"Oh," she whispered, nodding her head. "So um, what's up with Theresa?" I laughed so hard at her that she had to laugh herself.

"She's with Reggie," I told her, trying to laugh it off.

"That dirty lil' boy you insisted on hanging out with?" She wasn't laughing anymore. "That's not who she's pregnant by, is it?" I nodded and Mama shook her head. "What's wrong with her?" I laughed again and Mama got up to start dinner.

The rain had stopped and I went out on the porch, even though it was muggy and sticky outside. A group of girls laughed as they walked across the street. A short year ago, that had been Kim, Theresa, Tasha and I. The four of us had been through way too much to be so young. When Tasha pulled up, I was wondering what kinds of things Mama had done at our age.

"Hey, where's my lil' buddy?" I asked, referring to Kim's son, Isaiah.

"His bad butt is at home drivin' his mama crazy. Where's my god-daughter?"

"Upstairs asleep with her daddy."

"Oh, so Aaron moved on in, huh?" Tasha teased.

"Mama lets him spend the night every night but won't officially call it moving in. He has his own drawer and towel and toothbrush…"

"You need to stop." She was buggin' up. "So he can't live here, he can just spend the night for weeks at a time."

"I decided to leave it alone."

"So I heard from your friend," she said. I was quiet, so she kept going. "Why didn't you tell me you hit that girl in the face?"

"Oh, she was quick to call you and tell you that, but she didn't tell you she yelled out my business to the whole gas station. And you know the gas station is always packed."

"What business?"

"When she said I was with Reggie and Aaron in the same

day, I was heated, but not enough to hit her. Then she had the nerve to yell out that I slept with my father that day too. *That's* when I hit her."

"No- she- didn't!" Tasha's hand flew over her mouth. "What the hell were ya'll arguing about in the first place?"

"Oh, so I guess while she was crying that I abused her, she didn't tell you who her baby daddy is?" Tasha shook her head in suspense. "It's *Reggie*."

"Aw *hell* naw!" She put her hand on her mouth again. "It was bad enough when *you* were with him, but for her to get with him *too*…" She made gagging noises.

"Ya'll can't find anything better to do than gossip?" Aaron was in the doorway with JaLea.

"Whatever." Tasha waved him off. "I'm goin' for a ride. Ya'll wanna come?"

"Why would I wanna ride with ya'll gossiping all day?" he answered. I ran in to say bye to Mama and kissed Aaron and JaLea before hopping in with Tasha. Before I knew it, we'd laughed and talked our way all the way down Grand Ave. to the North Side.

"I didn't know I wanted some chicken until we got here." Tasha said. I laughed as she pulled into a *Church's* lot.

"Get me a two-piece!" I yelled as she walked toward the fast food joint. It was rowdy on the North Side, as usual. A homeless couple was posted outside the check cashing place begging for money. I watched them ease over to *Church's* to beg for chicken.

The Blumeyer projects towered behind the small strip of stores on Grand. I remembered going there once with Mama when one of her sisters stayed there. We had to hike up to the eighth floor in a piss-scented stairwell because the elevator was broken. My aunt didn't tell us she was clean out of food. Ten minutes later, we were walking back down the musty, stained stairwell because no one delivered to the projects.

"Here, hungry." I was in a daze until Tasha shoved a bag at me through the open window.

"I told you I didn't know she was yo girl!" a voice yelled from across the lot.

"Nigga you saw me with her last week." Tasha and I stared out the front window at the two guys arguing outside the apartments. We had front row seats and ate our chicken as we watched the drama unfold.

"Hey, it's not my fault yo girl gave it up that easy."

"I can't really see either one of their faces, but the boyfriend looks fresh and clean and the one the girl cheated with is dusty." Tasha smacked on her biscuit. I laughed but agreed with her. The boyfriend's clothes made the other guy look like he shoulda been standing with the couple outside *Church's*. "Girl… he look like Aaron, don't he?" She was pointing towards the dirty one and I shoved her arm.

"Please, my man is *too* fine to play around like that!" We had stopped listening and weren't paying attention when the shots rang out. Fries and chicken flew in the air and I counted five shots as we threw ourselves to the floor. When we heard a car peeling off, we eased our way back up into our seats. The boyfriend was gone and the other guy was lying on the ground a little ways past the check cashing place with his feet facing us. Curiosity drew me out of the car. Tasha was behind me on her cell phone with the police.

"There's been a shooting on Grand and Franklin at the Blumeyers." I was pretty sure I was looking at the second dead person I'd ever seen. I rounded the body a ways from his feet. Moving my eyes up slowly, I saw one bullet hole in his right thigh… two in his chest…

"Kyra! Get the hell away from him!" I heard Tasha but I couldn't move. Even with two bullet holes distorting his face, I could see plain as day that it was Reggie.

"Kyra, I said get away from him! We gotta go- *now*!"

A crowd was gathering and, through blurred vision, I watched the sidewalk shift into white carpet. *No, no… please no!!* I couldn't take my eyes off the gaping wounds in his face as the blood began to puddle around his head.

"*You- killed- me…*" Reggie managed to gurgle. I slapped my hands over my ears and shook my head violently, backing myself into the side of the check cashing place. By that time, it seemed like every tenant had migrated from the high rise apartments to the parking lot. And there I was, looking like the crazy person who was responsible.

"Gotdamnit. Kyra!" Tasha power walked over to me, trying her best not to look at the body. I pointed at him with a shaky finger.

"Move your feet and come on!" she yelled, pulling at my shirt.

"*Reggie…*" I whispered. Tasha stopped short and looked, then turned quickly away.

"Damn, *Reggie.*" She shook her head and wiped a hand across her forehead. "How old was he Kyra?" I turned back towards the street before answering.

"Seventeen."

THIRTEEN

Theresa didn't believe Tasha when she told her how the shooting unfolded. She didn't want to believe Reggie got killed by the boyfriend of a girl he was cheating on her with while she was pregnant. I sat silent on the couch, still stunned, even as she attacked me.

"Oh, so I guess you just *happened* to be all the way on the *North Side*! You couldn't handle the fact that everybody you get with ends up getting tired of you and wanting me instead. You probably had something to do with it!" I ignored her as gruesome images of blood seeping out of Reggie's bullet holes flashed through my mind. I couldn't tell if she was more upset at the fact that Reggie was dead or pissed because I'd been there.

***

The funeral was five days later. Mama and Aaron showed up merely for support. I knew neither one of them were particularly fond of Reggie. Tasha sat behind us near the middle of the church and I'd noticed Theresa in the very back row.

Afterwards, I gave Reggie's mother my condolences. I wanted to console her with thoughts of a soon-to-be grandchild until Theresa walked up acting as though I wasn't even there. It was painfully obvious, with the formal handshake and apology, that they'd never met. To Reggie's mother, Theresa was just another one of his female friends paying her respects. I thought about JaLea at Aaron's parents' house and felt sorry for Theresa and her unborn child.

***

I didn't want to get out of bed. It was July first, a year to the day I killed my father. With the exception of the day Reggie was shot, I hadn't had any illusions since JaLea was born. I noticed Aaron wasn't lying beside me and JaLea wasn't in her bed. I started down the stairs, half expecting the smell of Mama's bacon and eggs to waft into my nostrils. There were no smells, no cooking noises in the kitchen, no T.V., no voices… Where the hell was my family?

As I reached the bottom of the steps on my way to the kitchen, something in the living room caught my eye. There was a head sticking up over the back of a lounge chair I hadn't seen in a year. I kept telling myself I was dreaming, that my mind was playing this horrible nightmare again.

All of a sudden, I was watching myself tearing through the front door and into the kitchen. When I saw the knife, I knew I was reliving that day. I tried yelling, tried to make it stop, but no sound came out. I dragged myself towards the living room, not wanting to see the ugly scene play itself out, but not knowing what else to do. As soon as I got to the living room, the knife was jamming into his chest. I was being strangled and it was too late to run away. I couldn't turn away as I shook… "What the hell!" Aaron shoved me from the floor.

"What are you doin' down there?" I asked, wiping sleep from my eyes.

"You were screamin' and I tried to wake you up started swingin' and kicked me out the damn bed!" He yelled, pulling himself up. Any other day it would've been funny. I already knew what Aaron would say after I told him about my dream. *It's the anniversary*, he rationalized. *It was just a dream*, he said. I told him what happened the day Reggie was killed. *You were traumatized*, he told me. My own little psychiatrist.

By noon, Mama still wasn't up and about, which was unnatural for her. Peeking in her bedroom, I spotted her in the window sill, knees folded under her chin with her arms wrapped around her legs. I could tell she'd been crying and I wondered if it was because my father was dead, because I was the one who killed him, or both. I never did hear what happened to the body. Mama had told them to burn him and throw him in the trash. What if they had? It wasn't such a stretch. Why would anyone care about my penniless father?

Mama turned and looked dead at me through the slit between the door and the wall. I'd stepped on a creaky floorboard and I knew she heard me but I slowly pulled the door closed. I decided to avoid her as much as possible.

Aaron was washing JaLea up when I got back to the room. He said we didn't need to be cramped in the house all day. But I was scared out of my mind. Scared of being inside or out, scared of my dreams, scared of what Mama was thinking. Scared of my guilt engulfing me like Hiroshima's atomic bomb.

"It's real nice out..." Aaron rambled on, but I wasn't listening. It was all coming back to me, how he would beg me and tell me all the things Mama wouldn't do for him. *Let me get that other hole. It's tight, not like ya mama's. You know this is our little secret right?* I remembered getting in trouble for jamming a chair under my door knob. *You tried to lock me out? Now I gotta make you bleed.* And he had, all over my lavender sheets. I washed them when I was sure he and Mama were fast asleep. I tried my best to consider myself a virgin when my father started coming into my room, but, after that night, it was hard.

"You think she'll like the zoo?" Aaron was still talking.

"I don't know, I guess." Aaron had dressed JaLea in her yellow sundress, white sandals and white hat with yellow flowers. As happy as I was to have Aaron and our daughter, thoughts still lingered in the back of my mind. What if my *father* had turned out to be the father of my baby? Would I still love her the same? What if Reggie had been the father? Would I have

69

cried at the funeral? Would I be on my way to the zoo with Aaron if *he* wasn't the father?

"Put some clothes on, I still gotta get ready." He kissed my cheek and popped me on my butt. I giggled as I ran to shower, trying my best to forget the dead who lingered in my mind. I made sure the water was as hot as I could stand before I stepped in. I closed my eyes and pictured my baby. My daughter in her little dress with her big floppy hat. She was so beautiful and Aaron and I were lucky to have her. Just then, the water became disgustingly sticky. I opened my eyes and saw red and immediately closed them back. A skin peeling stench danced through my nostrils.

"*You- killed- me…*"

"Not today." I growled angrily. I opened my eyes and the blood was gone. *Not today*, I told myself. *I have to take my daughter to the zoo.*

FOURTEEN

"Theresa's at the hospital," Tasha said before I could get out a hello.

"Is she okay?" I was almost surprised at my concern as I repositioned the phone.

"She had the baby." There was a slight pause. "You're coming with me, right?" I didn't know what to say. Theresa had slept with two of my boyfriends, gotten pregnant by one, told my business, and blamed me for Reggie's death.

"I don't know, Tasha."

"Kyra!"

"Okay." I wanted to be there for Theresa but I felt like she didn't deserve the time it took to ride to the hospital, let alone my friendship. I loved her to death, but in the past year it seemed like she had tried her best to hurt me.

***

Theresa's mother was overly happy to see us. She showered us with bear hugs since she hadn't seen us in a while.

"I'm so glad you girls came. She really needs to be with her friends." I thought to myself, as Theresa's mother rambled on, how oblivious she was to the things her daughter had done. She knew nothing about why Tasha and I hadn't been around. "Go in, go in," she urged. Tasha went in easily but I lingered at the door. I wasn't 100% sure what I was feeling. There was, of course, hate and anger. I was nervous as hell and didn't know why, but I was also proud of her because I knew how hard childbirth could be. Somewhere, far in the back of my mind, I thought I felt a small bit of jealousy and that pissed me off. What the hell was I jealous for, because Theresa had Reggie's baby? I didn't want Reggie's baby, and was happy as hell that JaLea wasn't his.

"Aww, Kyra come look at him," Tasha said, leaning over the baby. He was tiny and yellow at 6 lbs. 4 oz. Jet black curls peeked out from under his little hat but he was asleep and I couldn't see his eyes. "What's his name?' Tasha asked. Theresa kept her eyes focused out the window on the darkening sky, lost in her own thoughts as if she were alone. Tasha and I looked at each other and shrugged our shoulders. "Bye Baby Boy Sanders." Tasha called before we left. I didn't want to bring up the fact that, even though the baby was cute, he didn't look like Reggie or Theresa.

***

"So does the baby look like me?" I guess Aaron called himself joking after I settled in back at home.

"No," I tried to snap at him but I was playing with JaLea. "But he doesn't look like Theresa or Reggie either." I tried to sneak a peek at his reaction. He just shook his head and kept on watching ESPN.

A week later the phone rang at a little past midnight. Irritated, I rolled over and looked at the caller I.D. *Theresa Sanders*. What in the hell could she possible want?

"Hello?" I tried to sound like I'd been asleep for hours even though I'd just gotten JaLea to sleep.

"I messed up." I could tell she'd been crying.

"What did you do?" I almost didn't care. I was sleepy and didn't feel like talking about Aaron, Reggie, or what used to be our friendship. After the way she'd acted towards me and Tasha at the hospital, I should've hung up on her.

"He wouldn't go to sleep. He wouldn't stop crying." I sat up.

"Theresa, what did you do?"

"I didn't mean to hurt him. I only shook him a little. He wouldn't *shut up!*"

"Gotdamnit Theresa!" I was pulling pants out of the dirty clothes. "Is he breathing?"

"I don't know."

"Call the police." I hung up on her, not expecting her to dial, so I called 9-1-1 myself. I had to call Tasha three times before she answered.

"I'm on my way," was all she said. I shook Aaron to let him know what was going on just in case I wasn't home when everyone woke up. Tasha was just pulling up when I ran out the front door.

"What is going on? You don't just call me after midnight ordering me to take you to see somebody you don't even like."

"She shook her baby." I wanted to cry thinking about the helpless newborn I'd seen at the hospital.

Tasha hesitated before replying. "So are we taking him to the hospital?"

"I don't know, I guess. I called the police already."

"You *what!*" The car swerved a little. "They're gonna take that baby from her! And where the hell is Theresa's mama?"

"I don't know." I sank into the seat. I hadn't thought about the police taking Theresa's baby. I felt like an asshole. She'd called me for help and I snitched on her.

Tasha turned onto Miami St. and my chest tightened at the sight of the flashing lights. I didn't want to think that the baby I knew only as 'Baby Boy Sanders' had been shaken to death. We hopped out of the car just as Theresa's mother was apparently being dropped off from a date. Maybe it wasn't clear to her that, while she was out enjoying a night on the town, her 16-year-old may need help with her week old newborn..

"Oh my God! What's going on!" she screamed. *You would know if you'd been home with her!* Tasha and I leaned against her car waiting to see Theresa. It wasn't long before we saw the stretcher. I took that as a good sign. I couldn't see the baby but I knew he was still alive because they were working on him. Theresa came lagging out behind them and her mother started in on her.

"What did you do to my grandson!? What the hell is wrong with you?" Theresa's expression was dull and unfeeling as Tasha and I moved in on her.

"Want us to take you to the hospital?" Tasha asked. Theresa was obviously in no hurry to get to the ambulance. She looked up from the ground slowly. Before she could reply her mother opened her mouth again.

"No she will not ride with you. She's gonna get her fast ass in *my* car and ride with me so she can tell me what the hell happened to that baby." I acted like I didn't even hear her.

"Do you want a ride Theresa?" I asked again.

"Didn't you hear me? I said she's coming with me!" Even as her mother said this, Theresa was moving towards Tasha's car. "Get your ass back over here!" Instead, Theresa quietly opened the back door and got in. Tasha and I followed, leaving Theresa's mother cursing and lunging her insults at the rear window.

She arrived at the hospital shortly after the three of us. I was on the verge of hating hospitals, and the uneasiness in the waiting room was not helping. The ride to Children's Hospital was a quiet one. Once we got there, Theresa sat silently looking at her fingers. Her mother sat across from us still dressed in her skin tight black dress with a deep v-cut neckline and her black three inch heels. Her arms and legs were crossed with her right foot swinging, and I could hear her sucking her teeth over the noise of the busy emergency room. She looked like she wanted to dig her fake nails into all three of us.

I wished that Theresa wasn't sitting between Tasha and me. It was apparent from the last few encounters I had with her, that Theresa no longer saw me as her friend. She could call me when she was in a bind but didn't have two words to say to me otherwise. I wanted to tell Tasha I was ready to go. What the hell were we doing there anyway, keeping Theresa's mama out of her face? I figured she didn't need us there, but I looked at her and she was in a pitiful daze. I wouldn't dare bring myself to be as ignorant as she had been. I wouldn't leave her while her son was in the hospital. I knew Tasha wouldn't either.

We all saw the doctor coming toward us and I immediately focused on the woman next to him. She was tall and dressed in a business suit with a tight bun at the nape of her neck. They stopped short of us and, even though Theresa didn't look up at him, the doctor told Theresa her baby would be fine.

She only twiddled her fingers a little faster when the woman introduced herself as a worker from the Division of Family Services.

FIFTEEN

I couldn't let JaLea out of my sight. I'd learned that Terrell, 'Baby Sanders', would be taken away. Not just away from Theresa, but out of the house period. He would stay with D.F.S. while Theresa's paternal grandparents fought for custody of him. Theresa had been sent to a program for teen mothers with post-partum depression. Her mother was lucky to have escaped jail time since both Theresa and her son were minors under her guardianship. After all, she hadn't actually been home when the incident occurred.

JaLea lay on her pallet on the floor kicking her chubby legs and paying no attention to the toys suspended from the pole above. I would never understand Theresa's situation. I adored my daughter and I'd rather leave her alone in her crib crying for an hour. Anything to keep from putting my hands on her. Then again, I had Mama and Aaron who helped whenever I needed them. Who did Theresa have? Her mama seemed clueless and if Reggie had been alive he probably wouldn't have been much help.

"Aaron's on the phone." Mama said poking her head in the door. I'd been daydreaming and hadn't heard the phone ring.

"Hello?"

"Hey, you got clothes on?"

"Yeah, why?"

"You know my uncle is barbequing today. You want my pops to come get you and JaLea?"

"Yeah, we're ready." I was more than happy to get out of

the house. All I needed to do was comb my baby's thick hair.

***

I'd never been alone with Aaron's father so the ride to the barbeque was quiet and a little uncomfortable. I was relieved when we finally made it to the party. Immediately, everyone crowded around to see JaLea. I was used to her getting all the attention. Besides, with everyone passing her around, Aaron and I had some time alone.

"I missed you last night," he told me once I finally found him sitting by the pool.

"I missed you too." I kissed him and plopped down in his lap.

"Where's my other baby?"

"You know they took her soon as I got here."

"Well, before you leave, everybody is gonna know who *you* are too."

"Is that right?" Before he could answer, someone stepped in front of us and blocked the sunlight.

"Hey lovebirds." The man was tall and bright-skinned with nappy hair on his face and the same hazel eyes as Aaron and JaLea. He was shirtless, showing off the sexiest chest and abs I'd ever seen. His wet trunks sat low, showing a tease of pubic hair, and they clung to him leaving nothing to the imagination. I felt myself blush and had to turn away.

"This is my uncle, Marcus." He stuck his hand out and I shook it.

"You must be Theresa." I yanked away and Aaron almost knocked me to the ground when he jumped up. Had his uncle just called me *Theresa*!?

"Marcus, what the hell!" Aaron was shoving his uncle and I was completely lost.

"I'm just playin' lil' mama. I know who you are… Kyra, Aaron's baby mama." He walked away, laughing and rambling to himself.

"Babe," Aaron reached out to me but I backed away from him. "Kyra," he called me again but I turned and headed for the house. I knew he wouldn't yell and bring attention to himself at his family barbeque. Once inside, I closed myself in the bathroom and tried to keep my tears quiet. His gotdamn uncle called me *Theresa*! I could care less whether he was joking around, drunk or whatever. Why did he know about that heffa in the first place? When dudes talked, they do it for bragging rights. Aaron wouldn't have told anyone about him and Theresa if he thought he'd so-called "fucked up" like he tried to convince me he had.

There was a soft knock at the door. "Kyra, please come out and let me talk to you." I wanted to yell *kiss my ass!* But I didn't know if there were people close enough to hear, so I kept my mouth shut. "Kyra, open the damn door." Now I knew there was no one in earshot.

"Tell me why I shouldn't come out there and kick your ass!"

"It's not even what you think…"

"Here we go with that again."

"Kyra come out."

"Yeah Kyra, come out." It was Marcus. He was really beginning to piss me off.

"Move, man. This is your fault." Aaron told him. I thought about Marcus then, how yellow he was. Then I thought about Theresa's son. He was just as yellow and looked nothing like Reggie or Theresa. Then again, he didn't look like Aaron or Marcus either. Without having seen the baby's eyes, there was no way to be a hundred percent sure who Terrell looked like. Reggie could have yellow people in his family…

"Marcus is gone Kyra. Can you come out now?" I reluctantly opened the door.

"I don't wanna do this right now Aaron. Go get my daughter. I wanna go home."

"No. I wanna tell you what's up so you won't be pissed at me." I folded my arms and leaned against the wall. *This should be good.* "While you were pregnant when I wasn't at your house, I was here. Marcus got on my nerves asking about you and why you were never around. One day I finally told him what happened wit' Theresa and why we weren't together. He laughed at me but I didn't think anything else of it." I rolled my eyes. "Marcus is an asshole and he likes to start shit. Plus, he's drunk as hell. He was drinkin' all night gettin' ready for the barbeque and he's been drinkin' all day." I looked up at him and those hazel eyes had me. *Damn!* Was I being dumb as hell? Had Aaron and Theresa slept together more than the one time I knew about? Was Terrell really Aaron's baby? Was I just a sucker for love?

"Who is that?" A short, stubby woman walked up with JaLea in her arms. "Is that Mommy and Daddy?" she asked in an irritating baby voice. Aaron introduced me to his cousin. He made sure he introduced me to everyone that crossed our path and I tried my best to steer clear of Marcus. I was successful right up until nightfall.

"Hey, sexy. Are you enjoyin' yourself?" he asked. I looked past him but Aaron and JaLea were nowhere to be found. Marcus leaned in close and I could smell the beer and Jack Daniels on his breath. "You sure don't look sixteen." I tried walking away but he followed. I could hear him panting behind me. "Your friend knew how to ride *real* good. You look like you can do just as good if not better." I spun around and immediately saw how excited he was, thanks to his tight trunks. I couldn't even find the words. Thoughts ran through my head but none would come out. I kept telling myself he was lying, but what did he have to lie for? He was drunk, but did that make him think I'd be impressed? And if it was true, how did he get to Theresa?

"Kyra!" Aaron yelled at me like I'd done something wrong. He hiked JaLea up on his hip, charged toward us, took one look at my face and turned to Marcus. "What did you say to her?"

"Chill out man. I was only telling her about her horny lil' friend you sent over to me."

"You were trickin' Theresa!" I made a couple of heads turn and decided to pull Aaron to the side of the house. Marcus followed like an obedient puppy. "What the hell is going on Aaron?"

"Hey, hey," Marcus had another beer in his hand, even though he was near the point of falling over. "Don't talk to my nephew like that. He did you a favor. The lil' hoe wouldn't leave him alone after he dicked her down properly, so he sent her over to me." Aaron tried to hide his face behind JaLea's head. "I was more than happy to take her off his hands." Marcus took a swig of beer and swaggered away.

"You tried to trick Theresa off on your uncle? How old is he anyway?"

"I don't know baby. And I wasn't trying to trick Theresa, I was trying to get her off my back."

"And introducing her to your grown ass, ignorant uncle was the way to do that?"

"I- I wasn't thinking…"

"I know you weren't." I shook my head, unable to believe how stupid Aaron had been. The fact that Theresa actually followed suit and slept with the man didn't even surprise me.

"I'm telling your daddy to take us home." I swiftly took JaLea from him and went to look for his father. Maybe he'd follow me, maybe he wouldn't. At that point I didn't even care.

SIXTEEN

I had been dreading the first day of junior year. The tutor had successfully helped Tasha and I catch up but I wasn't exactly jumping for joy like our parents were. JaLea's daycare shuttle had already picked her up and I was sitting on the bed watching Aaron get dressed.

"Are you planning on doing something to your hair?" he asked, tightening his belt. I wanted to be stubborn as hell and not go to school. Tasha didn't care what people thought or said about her, she was going to school anyway. Me, on the other hand, I let what other people think go to my head. I couldn't help but wonder if everyone knew I'd missed school because I got too damn lazy and embarrassed when I was pregnant. I wondered if Theresa had ran her mouth off about things I thought I was confiding in a friend about.

"Kyra," Aaron stepped in front of me. "I don't wanna be late on the very first day." I quickly brushed my hair up in a ponytail. I really didn't care what I looked like but I knew I had to get up and go.

Jefferson High School hadn't changed at all in the year I'd missed. The line of students waiting to get through the metal detectors stretched all the way down the front steps and halfway across the yard. Aaron stood behind me with his arms around my waist. I weeded the freshmen out in an instant: skinny little girls trying to get attention by wearing tight miniskirts in August. I had to laugh at the ones who didn't fill their shirts and had flat boards where their butts should've been. I hoped the silly hoes had goose bumps on their coochies.

"Hey ya'll. What's up?" Aaron and I turned to see Theresa grinning from ear to ear.

"Hey Theresa," Aaron answered. I nudged him. What the hell was she trying to pull? Maybe the program she was in had brainwashed her or made her feel like she had to make amends. Either way, I didn't like her walking up on us like everything was okay. Like the previous summer hadn't even happened and we were just as tight as we'd always been.

"Feels good for the first day of school, huh?" she asked as the line inched forward. Aaron and I looked at each other confused as hell. It took a couple of minutes for Theresa to get the picture but, eventually, she went on her way. Aaron and I kissed before I headed to first period, English Literature. I had the nerve to have the most boring class early in the morning. Then I stepped in the door... and there was Theresa's cheery ass! She grinned, the same happy-go-lucky grin she'd given me outside, and patted the desk next to her. She was trippin'. I took a seat at the other end of the room near a window. By the time the bell rang, that hoe was sitting next to me. She talked my ear off the whole fifty minutes about irrelevant stuff she must've really thought I cared about.

Relief swept over me when the bell rang and I ran to the bathroom. Four girls startled me as I splashed water on my face. I recognized them as a group of bullies, but I'd never been bullied in my life so I wasn't trippin' as I attempted to step quietly past. The biggest one leaned against the door with her back and what looked like a size twelve Jodeci boot. She crossed her muscular arms as the other three stepped in front of her. Big Hair, Yellow Teeth and Flat Chest... I'd never taken time to learn their names, but they all donned huge boots and ridiculously baggy clothes.

"Slept with anybody's daddy lately?" Yellow Teeth spit out. The other three roared with laughter and I squinted my eyes as my head began to spin.

"Heard you got a lil' incest baby too." Flat Chest added her two cents. They kept spitting insults at me but I couldn't hear them anymore. The only thing going through my head was how bad I wanted to kick Theresa's ass. She had to have been the only one running her mouth. I pushed past Big Hair trying to get to the door but the one with the size twelve boots kicked me in my side. It felt like my lung collapsed and Flat Chest shoved me into the nearest sink. As I doubled over in pain, I saw my daughter's face and told myself I'd be damned if I let those big bitches take me down. I looked each one of them dead in the eyes.

"Oh, you got balls now," Size Twelve shouted.

"What you gonna do?" Yellow Teeth asked. "Stab us?" They all busted out laughing again and my nerves got the best of me as I ran into a stall. That didn't keep them from harassing me and pounding on the door.

"Ladies!" I recognized Mrs. Burton's voice. "Shouldn't we be in second period?"

"Yes Ma'am," they sang in unison. It was amazing how their attitudes changed. I listened as the group filed obediently out of the bathroom. I wished, unsuccessfully, Mrs. Burton would leave too.

"Are you okay?" She asked. I opened the door and brushed past her. "Kyra…"

"I'm fine." I cut her off and kept walking. I had no way of knowing if she knew all my business too. All I knew was I'd been at school for an hour and was ready to go. I hoped, as I crept down the back steps, that the basement was still camera free.

There was no light at all so I slowed down a little as I descended. I could smell that basement smell and had the distinct feeling I should've turn around. I searched the corners of my mind to remember the layout of the basement. It had been a while since the last time Tasha, Theresa and I had skipped class there. I let memories take over as I ran my fingers along the dusty wall. My side ached and there were tears in my eyes thinking of what used to be. Then a hand clamped over my mouth.

My first thought was that the girls from the bathroom had followed me, but there was a disgusting, overpowering stench mixed with the funk of the basement. I tried spinning around but a huge arm swung in front of me pulling me back into an all too familiar body. My eyes bugged and I panicked in the pitch blackness. I began scratching at his hands, trying to pull them off me but dead skin gathered in my palms. I tried to scream through the hand over my mouth but it didn't work. I was tempted to give up, tired of living the guilt this way, tired of feeling like I was crazy and losing my mind. To make things even worse, I *knew* none of it was real. I knew my father was dead and he wasn't in the basement holding me hostage, but I couldn't control what was going on in my head.

"You-killed-me..." *So damn what! I did it and you deserved it you bastard!* Then he flung me from his grasp, right out of the basement door into the blinding sunlight.

SEVENTEEN

"What the hell happened to you?" Aaron asked, half yelling, when he got home from school. He was pissed and threw his backpack into the wall. "You weren't at lunch, Tasha ain't seen you, Theresa's crazy ass was even lookin' for you! I waited after school for hella worrying my ass off and here you are laid up in the bed lookin at *Maury*!" I laughed and gripped my side, trying to hide the grimace of pain. "Ain't nothin' funny Kyra." Aaron sat on the bed beside me. "You know I'm telling yo mama right?"

"What!" I sat straight up, which was a mistake, and winced as I eased back down.

"What's wrong with you?'

"Nothin'."

"Don't lie to me Kyra." I thought back and wondered if I had ever lied to Aaron. I couldn't think of a time when I had, especially when it came to my hallucinations. But I just wanted them to go away. I didn't want to talk to Aaron or anybody else about my problems anymore. It seemed to make them all the more real. "Kyra." Aaron was still waiting for his answer.

"The big girls with the boots caught me in the bathroom." He searched his mind to figure out who I was talking about, then his eyes widened.

"*Those* girls? What the hell for? What happened?"

"I don't know who Theresa was running her mouth off to, but those girls knew all my business. And they threw it in my face."

"What did they do?" Aaron's voice was softer now.

"They just pushed me around a little until Mrs. Burton came in and scared them off."

"But nobody talks to them, they only hang out with each other. If they know, then who else knows?"

"Exactly. That's why I left. No telling who's looking at me and what they're thinking. They even said JaLea was his."

"Who's? your dad's?" he asked. I nodded. Aaron would've been disgusted just thinking JaLea was someone else's, let alone my father's. "Where the hell did they get that from?"

"You know how mixed up stuff gets when people pass rumors. No telling what Theresa's sayin'."

"Seriously though, you still gotta go to school."

"Fuck school!" I was livid at that point, thinking about Theresa and her big mouth. "Fuck Theresa and whoever else that thinks they know enough about what's goin on in my life to talk about it."

"Calm down." I guess since he was so calm he expected me to be. It wasn't his name being dragged through the mud. It wasn't his side that was hurting from almost getting jumped. And he wasn't the one being haunted by a dead man. But I calmed down anyway. No use trying to make him understand.

***

For the rest of the week, Aaron acted as my personal bodyguard. He met me after each class and walked me to my next one, even if it made him late. Luckily, my first period teacher had given us assigned seats so Theresa was sitting nowhere near me. She did, however, manage to find me and Tasha at lunch. Neither one of us paid her much attention but she didn't seem to mind. She rambled on anyhow.

I was at ease with how things were going until Friday during fifth period when I got a note that Mrs. Burton wanted to see me. I always saw the counselor as my 'school mama' because she was so cool, but I still didn't feel like going over the past with her. It was the past and I was desperately trying to put it behind me. My heart pounded and as my heels tapped against the linoleum, I realized how quiet it was, how alone I was in the hall. I started running, suddenly eager to get to Mrs. Burton's office. I was panting and out of breath by the time I knocked, but she didn't seem to notice.

"Kyra," she answered with a smile. "I hoped you'd come." I flashed my own fake smile back at her and sat down, dreading the conversation to come. "So, do you want to talk about last summer?" Damn, she didn't waste time, did she? *Hi Kyra. How are you, Kyra?*

"I had a rough patch." was all I said, but deep down I knew she had heard something.

"Did what I witnessed in the bathroom the other day have anything to do with your rough patch?" I struggled for a moment, wondering if I should lie. Instead, I just nodded my head. "To my understanding, there were a lot of things that contributed to your rough patch." She clasped her slender high yellow fingers and looked dead into my eyes. Something made me want to tell her the truth, but I knew I couldn't. What would be the point? She obviously knew something and I was beginning to think she was using her status to be nosy. What could she possibly have been trying to do besides get the goods straight from the source?

"Last summer my father died and I was pregnant this past school year but I caught up with a tutor."

"I'm sorry about your father's death." There was disbelief in her eyes and I knew she'd heard it through the grapevine that it was no 'accidental' death. Now I wanted to know how long it would take her to tell me she knew the truth. "Have you fully recovered from his… *death*?" Was she trying to be funny? What was the pause for?

"It was over a year ago. I've recovered." I heard the

attitude in my voice and I wondered if she caught it. I'd always thought she was so pretty with her flowing, sandy brown hair and long legs. She kept herself dressed and all the dudes were always in her face no matter how much she laughed at them and turned them away. Now here was my 'school mama' all in my business and pissing me off. She looked at me for a minute, I guess trying to plan her next move since I wasn't caving.

"What about your child? How is she developing?"

"Beautifully." She nodded and grinned a little.

"I'd love to meet her sometime. What's her name?"

"I'm sure you know already." Her eyes narrowed. "Just like you know everything else." She sat back in her chair, obviously stunned, and I waited until she opened her mouth to speak so I could purposely cut her off. "By the way, how *do* you know everything else?" I figured she wouldn't tell me, but I could at least watch her stutter for a lie.

"Kyra! Why would you assume…"

"I don't have to assume. Why did you call me in here if you didn't know anything?"

"I've been very concerned about you."

"Yeah, but why?"

"Being a teenage mother can be very traumatic."

"Okay, what about last summer? Why ask about that?" She was stuck. I guess she never expected me to have such an attitude. She thought I'd just open up to her because of who she was. Well she was dead wrong.

"I've heard some things," she started. "I didn't want to just believe what I heard. And after what I saw on Monday…" her voice trailed off and she looked genuinely concerned, but she'd just admitted she was being nosy. Not in those exact words, but I knew she wanted to know the truth to quench her own curiosity.

"Half of what you heard is most likely true." I grinned a little, wondering if she was trying to decipher what was the truth and what was a lie. She started looking a little irritated, like she was tired of me playing games with her. I really didn't give a care.

"If you need to talk, I'm here for you." *She'd be there by her damn self.*

"Thank you," I told her and left.

EIGHTEEN

Tasha had the nerve to show up at my house with Theresa. I almost dropped JaLea when I saw the two of them on the porch. I hesitated for a moment, cursing Tasha for not giving me a heads up.

"Hey," I put on a happy face when I opened the door.

"Hey," they said in unison.

"Somebody wants to talk to you." Tasha motioned toward Theresa. I wondered, in the two months that school had been in, why Theresa hadn't approached me herself. Instead, she'd rambled on about nonsense making me think she was crazy.

"I wanna clear the air about… things." I had to catch myself. It had been over a year since I caught Theresa and Aaron together and it was hard to believe things could've gotten any worse between us, but they had. And then, after everything, from our kids, to my father and Reggie, she wanted to bring up things I'd tried long and hard to forget. I let them in anyway.

"Where's Aaron?" She wasn't going in the right direction if she was trying to 'clear the air'. Tasha saw the look on my face and stepped in.

"She just wants to make sure we can talk without being interrupted." I told them he was at the gym and took JaLea up to lay her down.

"Does she have a nursery?" Theresa asked when I got back to the living room.

"She's got her own little space in my room."

"That's nice. How's your mom? Is she here?"

"She's fine. She's at the grocery store."

"So we got about an hour alone?" I nodded, tired of Theresa's small talk. The three of us sat in awkward silence, looking at each other like total strangers, until Theresa decided to talk.

"First off, I wanna apologize for bein' a asshole. I know ya'll probably hate me."

"We don't hate you, do we Kyra?" I wanted to tell Tasha to shut up and speak for herself, but I shook my head instead. Then Theresa started from the top and shocked the hell out of me.

"Once, when me and Tasha spent the weekend over here in seventh grade, I woke up real early in the morning to go to the bathroom. Somebody started coming in and I thought it was one of ya'll, but it was your daddy." My stomach jumped in my chest and I could feel Tasha tense up beside me. I knew what was coming and I didn't want to hear it but Theresa kept going anyway. "I hit my funny bone trying to rush and pull up my panties and shorts but he was already locking the door. He raped me, right there in the bathroom. He didn't say anything, he didn't make any noise. He just shoved a wet towel in my mouth, pushed me up against the sink, and made me bleed all over the floor, and left." She said it so nonchalantly and tears stung my eyes thinking of her going through the same hell I'd been through. Tasha got up and went over to sit beside her.

"Oh my God, Theresa why didn't you say something?" she asked her.

"The same reason Kyra didn't say anything. I was ashamed." Our eyes met and I was speechless. Tasha was looking back and forth, obviously confused.

"What's goin' on?" she asked. Theresa looked dead at her.

"I knew the day Kyra told us she killed that bastard that she was lying about what happened. No way was she living under this roof wit him and the same thing that happened to me didn't happen to her. She made it seem like that was the first time but that's B.S! The way I figure it, it had been happening for years. She knew how screwed up her father was and had us spending the night over here! She could've either told us the truth or not had sleepovers with her child molesting daddy sleepin across the hall. And she never even asked why I never spent the night again, did you Kyra?" She shot a glance at me. "Either way, if she would've been straight with us, we wouldn't have been over here for me to get raped in the first place." Tasha slowly turned towards me.

"Kyra, *why*?"

"I couldn't bring myself to say anything to anybody."

"That, I understand, but why did you have us spending the night? That's like me letting you drive my car without telling you the brakes are going out. Eventually, it's gonna backfire."

"I was always scared being here alone and…"

"So you brought over fresh new bait for your daddy?" Theresa cut me off.

"No! It wasn't like that at all. I never would've thought he'd have done something to one of you. I thought it was just me."

"If he did it to his own daughter then why would he think twice about doing it to one of us?" Theresa locked angry eyes with me for a moment the living room was deathly quiet.

"I'm sorry," was all I could say. Now I was the one who felt like an asshole. Theresa disregarded my apology and kept on with her story.

"After the truth finally hit me, I was pissed. I wanted to hurt you. I wanted to make you suffer for putting me in that situation then lying about it. Your only weak spot that I could think of was Aaron. It had nothing to do with us liking each other. I practically forced him and refused to leave, hoping you'd show up. I told Tasha I wanted him so bad because I knew eventually she'd tell you and you'd be even more hurt. I even started calling Aaron everyday trying to get on his nerves hoping he'd tell you. He told me he felt bad enough and to leave him alone. So I showed up at his house one day. He was there with his uncle, Marcus, and we ended up hookin' up. I was tired of being alone, tired of trying to talk Aaron into doing something he didn't wanna do, just to make you mad. So I went with it. I knew it was just sex, but I went with it anyway. Got pregnant a few months later and never heard from him again."

She paused and I took the chance to soak in everything she'd said. From what she told us, she thought I'd basically ruined her life by not telling her the truth about my father. I couldn't even look at her, thinking about all the feelings that came along with being raped. The pain, first and foremost, was indescribable. Then the humiliation, the anger, and the sheer disbelief that this… *person* is somebody you *know*. I knew what she felt, probably ten times over. But there was a difference. I contributed to her pain. And no doubt, she partly blamed her pregnancy on me, even though she'd chosen to sleep with Marcus. I forced myself to suppress my relief from hearing the truth about Aaron from her mouth, but I was still confused.

"What about Reggie?" I asked her.

"I saw Reggie on the way to the store that day and he ran his mouth about how dirty you were to him. I guess he just wanted to play with your head. I was thrown off at first with him actin' all nice like he was my baby daddy, but when I realized what he was doing, I played along. It got a little out of hand."

"I know. I'm sorry." The longer she talked, the worse I felt.

"Reggie was cool, but we never messed around. And when I had Terrell, I just wanted to be left alone but my mama got such a big mouth ya'll were there in no time. I couldn't stand looking at him. He reminded me of Aaron's uncle and I hated that. One night I just snapped. I know Terrell's okay with my dad's parents now, but I still feel bad. I don't know what I was thinking trying to talk to ya'll at school without having this conversation first, but now that I got everything off my chest, I just want my friends back."

Tasha was the first to hug her. I pulled myself over to the couch to hug her too, but some things were still bothering me. Theresa obviously had a lot of serious animosity towards me, which I understood. But where had it all gone? Why was she opening up now? Why had she told everybody my business?

"I gotta use the bathroom." Theresa excused herself.

"Well, that was… unexpected." Tasha said once she was sure Theresa was out of earshot. I could only nod. Theresa had completely blown me out of the water and she knew it. I felt so bad for wondering how much of it she'd embellished to make me feel worse. "I wonder what the hell went on at that home for teen mothers," Tasha thought aloud. I shrugged my shoulders, wondering the same thing.

"She's been gone a while, she better not be doing what I think she's doing in my bathroom." I tried to lighten up the mood a little as I got up to knock on the bathroom door. It was open so I figured she decided to stink up the upstairs. I started to laugh to myself and that's when I saw the kitchen patio door open. Letting the fear subside, I slid the door closed and headed upstairs. I stopped to check on JaLea and my whole body went limp.

The crib was empty.

I ran into the doorframe trying to get to the bathrooms on the second floor. Rage bubbled out in tears as I rushed through the house, finding each bathroom empty.

Finally, once I reached the stairs again, I was able to close my eyes, throw my head back, and scream at the top of my lungs. I knew Tasha was coming and I couldn't even bring myself to speak. All I could think was that when I got my daughter back from Theresa's ass, it would feel so good putting a knife in that crazy bitch's chest. I had done it once before, and for JaLea I'd do it again.

NINETEEN

I woke to Aaron's voice and thought it had all been a dream, but I was wrong. He was asking me if I was okay. Apparently, I'd passed out right before he got home. He told me he carried me down to the couch and not too long after, Mama had come home.

"Then she said she had to use the bathroom and I guess she slipped upstairs and snuck out the back with the baby." Tasha was hurriedly filling the two officers in as Mama sat staring at her with bewilderment. "I called her house like ten times but nobody answered." I sat up slowly, feeling like I'd failed JaLea and Aaron.

"I'm so sorry," I said, not to anyone in particular. "I should've known something was wrong."

"How could you have known?" Mama kneeled in front of me with tears in her eyes and the officers were at attention.

"Soon as she got here, she asked where you and Aaron were. She even asked how long we'd be alone claimin she didn't want us to be disturbed." I dug deeper into my memory and my heart sank even more. "She asked if JaLea had a nursery and I told her she was in my room." I was beating myself up inside. How could I have been so *stupid*? How could I let my daughter get kidnapped from right under my nose? I needed my ass beat almost as much as Theresa did. I thought again about what I would do to her once I got my hands on her. She had conned her way into my house to take my baby, and I would've loved nothing more than to put her scandalous ass in the ground. But I had to be smart. Otherwise, I could get JaLea taken away just like Theresa had gotten Terrell taken away. That was the last thing I wanted. I couldn't handle that. Wondering what she planned on doing with my daughter made me burst into tears. My heart was breaking and suddenly I felt sick... all over the white carpet.

Tasha went upstairs to get pictures of Theresa and JaLea and when Aaron came back with towels, I tried my best to help him clean up the mess. My body was weak from missing my baby and Aaron had to shake me out of a daze when the police wanted to question me. I briefly filled them in on the past year or so, trying to downplay the rapes, even though they were the dominating factor of the story. I could tell Mama was trying to conceal her feelings after realizing that my father had apparently raped Theresa too.

After they'd taken all their notes and a few pictures of Theresa and JaLea, the two officers left, promising to follow up on all their information and potential leads. The four of us looked around at each other, obviously irritated.

"They weren't helpful at all," Tasha blurted out. "They act like they can't do anything since JaLea's only been gone an hour."

"I say we find that lil' heffa ourselves," Mama said. Aaron, Tasha and I turned, stunned, to look at her. "What? She came in here and took my grandbaby and if those ignorant officers won't find her then we will." She was already pulling on her coat and we had to rush to catch her on her way out the door.

Tasha sat in the front seat jotting down the same list of leads we'd given the officers. The first stop, of course, was Theresa's house. There was no answer at the door so the four of us crept around peeking in the windows to see if any lights were on. No such luck. Mama called Ms. Sanders, Theresa's mother, on the way to her office at U.S. Bank. The rest of us listened intently.

"Yes, Margaret Sanders please... Hi Margaret, this is Danielle, Kyra's mom... Not too good actually. Have you heard from Theresa in the last few hours?" I leaned forward a little. "On her way to my house with Tasha, huh? Well, you know the girls have been having some problems. They got together to talk and now Theresa and JaLea are missing."

"Missing! What do you mean missing?" It wasn't hard to hear Theresa's mom through the cell phone and, after another minute or so, Mama hung up.

"She wants me to meet her back at her house. She claims she wants to help." Mama made a u-turn. "We'll see how helpful she is when we tell her that her what's *really* goin on."

***

After we'd been sitting in front of the house for twenty minutes, Mama called U.S. Bank again only to learn that Ms. Sanders had left twenty five minutes earlier. We sat another ten minutes before deciding she really wasn't coming.

"Now what?" Aaron asked, breaking the silence. Tasha flipped through her notepad.

"Well they sent her son to stay wit her dad's parents on Jefferson but I don't know the address." Mama called information, and, in seconds, we were headed to the home of Charles and Etta Williams. When we got there, we all got out of the car hoping the couple would be able and willing to shed a little light on the situation. A handsome man answered the door and, even though I'd never met Theresa's father, I knew that had to be him.

"Can I help you?" he asked, scanning the four or us suspiciously. Mama spoke up.

"I'm Danielle Conner and this is my daughter..."

"Kyra," he finished her sentence. His face hardened and I felt the tears building up. *He knows something.* "Please, come in." He moved to the side and let us step into the lavish entry hall. Huge elephant ears sat in a corner beside a plush, red cherry wood lounging chair. Four decorative scenic pictures hung in gold frames on the cream-colored walls and a rug sat in the middle of the floor. It was round and deep red with intricate gold details, and if I didn't know better, I would've sworn white people lived there.

Theresa's grandparents met us in the hall and, after introductions, we followed them into the living room. It was just as gaudy as the foyer with overstuffed furniture, giant plants, expensive looking rugs and pictures of everything but family. I was tense and uncomfortable, but determined to get all the information out of them that I could.

"Why don't you tell us what's going on young lady?" I held back a scream as Theresa's grandfather focused on me. *If you know something damnit, tell me!*

"Theresa and our friend Tasha came to my house to talk. She lied about having to use the bathroom and snuck out the back door with my daughter." Their facial expressions didn't waver one bit. *They already knew.*

"Why would she do that?" her father asked, seemingly uninterested. What the hell was wrong with them? Theresa's son was taken from her and placed in their home and their asking me why she did it! But what if they already knew and were just waiting for me to admit how I'd so-called ruined her life?

"Charles, can't you see this young woman has been traumatized enough by your demon spawn?" Theresa's grandmother cut in. Aaron tried to stifle a laugh and I nudged him in the side. "Kyra, sweetie I don't know where Theresa is, but we received a note from her. She must have slipped it under the front door a couple of hours ago." The woman got up and moved to a side table where she took a folded piece of paper out of the drawer. "As soon as I read it, I told my husband and called Theresa's parents. Her mother sounded quite disturbed but never showed up. We've been scared to call the police. I trust you do understand. After all, she *is* our granddaughter." She forced a small grin. *And your granddaughter shook the hell out of her own baby and put him in the hospital!*

    I took the paper from her outstretched hand and had to keep from getting sick all over their carpet too. Aaron was beside me asking to read the letter but I had to read it over again just to make sure I wasn't trippin. It read:

Guess what Grandma and Grandpa,
I'm not lonely anymore.
I was hurt at first because ya'll took my baby from me.
But I got another one so I'm good now.
Oh, and tell Kyra- because I know you'll talk to her-
that I said thank you. I wanted a girl anyway.
Love, Theresa

TWENTY

I was weak as the letter was being passed around. There had been times when I thought I was going crazy, but Theresa was far more gone than I was. People around me were talking but the words were going in one ear and out the other. Was all of this my fault? Had I set the ball rolling when I let my friends spend the night knowing how my father was? Would they have understood how and why the abuse went on for so long? I wanted to blame it all on my father. I didn't want to believe that I could've saved my daughter three years ago by just opening my mouth.

"What did her mother say when you called?" Mama asked Mrs. Williams.

"The conversation was a short one. I asked her had she heard from Theresa and she snapped a little. She told me no, but it seemed like she had to me. She was quick with her answers and told me she'd be here as soon as she was able to leave. That was an hour ago." I couldn't help but think that she knew exactly where her daughter was.

"Can you think of anywhere or anyone else your daughter would go for comfort?" Mama asked Theresa's father.

"My daughter and I haven't been close in years. I have no idea where she'd be. And if I did I wouldn't be wasting my time here would I?" I wanted to slap him.

"Well, in that case," Mama stood, obviously as irritated as I was. "I'll leave my cell number here and if you hear anything please don't hesitate." She paused at the thought of Theresa's father's attitude, and gave the number to her grandmother instead. Just then, a thought hit me.

"Mama, do the police have your cell phone number?" By the way she looked at me I could tell they didn't. We said our goodbyes and thanked the grandmother, since she was the only one who'd been helpful, and packed ourselves back into the car.

"Please Lord, let there be a message on the machine," Mama prayed silently to herself. I slumped against Aaron's shoulder and looked at my watch. It had been almost two hours since Theresa took JaLea. I wanted to think positively, but I didn't have much faith in the officers that had been at the house and we hadn't had any luck ourselves. I cried helplessly into Aaron's shoulder until we got home.

"The light's blinking!" Tasha yelled, pointing to the answering machine. We gathered around as Mama pushed the button.

"Danielle, this is Margaret," Theresa's mother sounded urgent. "Call me." We wasted no time filing back into the car while Mama dialed Theresa's house.

"Margaret!" she practically yelled. Aaron, Tasha and I were on pins and needles. Something big was happening; I could feel it in my heart. Aaron squeezed my hand like he could feel the same thing. "I'm on my way." Mama hung up the phone. "Theresa left her mama a letter too." I was antsy and practically bolted out of the car when we pulled up to the house not three minutes later.

"Kyra!" I had to bite my tongue when Theresa's mama answered the door and hugged me. When she let go, I slid past her to let the others in and waited for them in the living room. I was about to bust at the seams. This woman knew something that I didn't and she was wasting time greeting everyone. *You're not a hostess at a gotdamn party! Sit down and talk!* I noticed her eyes were dry and her facial expressions looked rehearsed.

At that point, I could've cared less. It didn't matter whether or not she knew what my father did to me, or that I killed him. I could care less what she thought about me. I didn't even care if she thought JaLea was my father's child and I was a hoe. I just wanted my daughter home.

"Shortly after you called me, I got a call from Theresa's grandparents. When they read the letter I got so upset I completely forgot I was supposed to meet you here. I drove around trying to figure out where she could be. When I got home I found this slipped under the front door." I almost snatched the letter from her.

God gave me another chance to prove I can be a good
mother- better than you anyway.
You're not even home when I need you.
There are other people I can talk to, you know.
Other people who take time out to listen to me.
Thanks for nothing.

She'd just been drivin' around wit my baby leavin' everybody notes like it was *normal*! I passed the letter around while thoughts scrambled in my head. It was becoming obvious that, not only did Theresa intend on paying me back, she thought she was going to be my daughter's mother. She didn't seem to want to hurt JaLea, but she hadn't intended on hurting Terrell either.

"Do either of you know who she could be confiding in? Other friends at school maybe?" her mother asked.

"We haven't talked to her in a while so we wouldn't know about her new circle of friends, or if she even has one," Tasha answered. I was wishing I'd paid more attention to her nonsense talk at lunch. There may have been a clue as to what the hell was going on in her head. I glared at her mother. It really was a shame she couldn't think of anything that would give even an inkling as to who else Theresa could've been talking to. I saw Mama fold the letter and put it in her pocket, getting up to leave.

"Thank you for all your help," she told Theresa's mother sarcastically. It felt like we'd wasted precious time and everyone was disappointed getting back into the car.

The ride home was quiet and depressing and we arrived to find that no more messages waiting for us. I plopped down on the couch feeling beat. We'd exhausted all our possibilities and had to resort to relying on the police. I didn't know where they'd gotten with their investigation. We had the letters Theresa wrote so there was nothing for the police to read whenever they decided to check the leads we'd given them. I started feeling sick to my stomach again, wondering if we had somehow helped Theresa by taking the letters without the police having read them. They probably wouldn't believe they were real since they hadn't found the letters themselves. I needed to do something. Post flyers, collect money for a reward... something. Just then, the phone broke the silence and I almost knocked Aaron off the couch trying to get it.

"Hello?" I felt in my gut that it was about JaLea.

"Kyra?" The voice on the other end was vaguely familiar and I felt my heart beating out of my chest.

"This is she," I answered. Aaron jumped up behind me and Mama and Tasha followed.

"This is Mrs. Burton." My shoulders sank and I almost hung up the phone thinking about our last conversation. What could she possibly want? "Theresa showed up here about twenty minutes ago with JaLea." I couldn't hold back the tears. I wanted to stay on the phone but my knees became weak and I fell to the floor.

"Who is this?" I heard Aaron demanding through my sobs. "What's your address?" His voice softened and I tried to calm down as Aaron told Mama and Tasha about the call. I was still crying fifteen minutes later when we pulled up in front of Mrs. Burton's house.

Aaron and I stood behind Mama and Tasha as we waited.

I hardly heard the introductions and I couldn't acknowledge Mrs. Burton when she spoke to me. All I knew was that my baby was in her house, and so was the heffa that took her.

"I played along with her to keep her here until I could get you on the phone, she whispered as we followed her down a narrow hall. "She claimed she wanted me to see her baby and I told her she could stay here until she found somewhere to go. Didn't take her long to fall asleep. I called her mother and the police after I called you but they haven't gotten here yet." She made a sharp right turn into what looked like a small living room. There was Theresa, asleep on the couch with a small, pink bundle beside her. I moved slowly with Aaron at my heels.

JaLea was awake and unharmed and it all felt so surreal. Aaron brushed past me and scooped her off the couch. He was crying and I realized that he hadn't cried at all that day. Now I was the one with the dry eyes. Mama and Tasha crowded around to see her too. Somehow, she seemed more beautiful than ever. Her skin was darker, her eyes more hazel, her dimples were deeper and her gummy grin was bigger. I was drawn to her until I saw Theresa stir out of the corner of my eye. She wasn't even fully awake before I swung, connecting with her face. Her head flung to the side and her eyes popped open in surprise.

"What the hell!" she yelled. I didn't even answer her. I just swung again. My only thought now that my daughter was safe was to beat Theresa's ass. After the second punch, she tried to get up and I pushed her back down by her face. I was surprised that no one was trying to stop me, not even Mrs. Burton. I cocked my fist to swing again but there was a knock at the door that stopped me from clocking her again. Mrs. Burton returned moments later with Theresa's mother and the police.

***

Christmas break had come and gone before Theresa was put on trial for kidnapping. Testifying and having lawyers go over my life with a fine-toothed comb was excruciating.

According to the prosecution, I was the innocent victim who'd had more than a tough life. The defense pegged me as the starting point of the downward spiral in Theresa's life. Oddly enough, my father, Theresa's parents, and even Theresa herself weren't blamed by the defense. It didn't matter though. Theresa was tried as an adult and sentenced to a minimum of seven years. Deep down I still wanted to stick my foot in her ass, but, instead, Aaron and I took our daughter home where she belonged.

PART THREE

consequences

TWENTY-ONE

I was so tired of walking through the mall but I couldn't leave. I shouldn't have waited until the last minute to get the rest of JaLea's birthday gifts. She already had her micros and outfit for her party. Thankfully, Tasha worked at the radio station and was able to talk a couple of deejays into coming. Plus, she bought a ridiculously large and expensive cake. I still needed to get JaLea's chain and her Jordan's. That brat had made out the most detailed birthday list I'd ever seen. The lil' heffa even thought she deserved a car just because she was turning sixteen. *Please*! All I had was a lil' Envoy myself. Besides, I'd already spent two-hundred on her hair and one-fifty on her outfit and I was about to drop another hundred on a pair of shoes and probably close to that on a damn chain. I must've been losing my mind.

After I spent another two-hundred at the mall, I headed home to finish setting up. By the time I got there, Aaron had already finished. It was nothing big really. He'd covered the couches in the den with light purple slip covers and hung purple and white streamers from the ceiling. He'd also mounted a small disco ball on a high shelf for effect. A few balloons were scattered on the floor and tables were set up for food. Mama was starting on the hot wings and Aaron was apparently resting from all his hard work.

"Hey Mama," I sat the bag down on the table and she looked in.

"Just because Aaron works in construction does *not* mean ya'll need to spoil that girl like this," she said.

"Mama, it's JaLea's sixteenth birthday and Aaron makes more than enough money to spoil the both of us." I gave her a big Eddie Murphy smile.

"A hundred twenty dollars on a pair of *shoes*, Kyra?"

"That's what she wanted." I snatched the bag off the table and went to put it up before Jalea got home. Aaron was laid out in the middle of the bed with his uniform on. He knew how much I hated that.

"Get up!" I hit his boot and he jerked awake. "The den looks good." He stirred and sat up rubbing his eyes.

"Thanks babe." He stood, stretched, and started undressing for a shower. I'd watched him grow from a boy to a man and Lord have mercy, construction had done his body good! His shoulders had broadened, his arms were more muscular, his thighs were thick and tight and his back was covered in tattoos. After seventeen years together and five years of marriage, he was still sexy as hell.

"Mama's downstairs cooking the chicken. Are you taking her home when she finishes?" He answered but I wasn't listening. I was paying too much attention to his nakedness. I wanted to reach out and touch somethin' but I heard JaLea come home. I'd have to settle for a couple of kisses until I could sneak him away during the party.

"Mama!" JaLea yelled as Aaron slipped into the master bathroom. After she knocked and I told her to come in, she stood in the middle of the floor flinging her braids everywhere. "How should I fix 'em for the party, Mama?" I couldn't help but stare at her. My baby was sixteen years old and I couldn't believe it. She'd grown into the spitting image of her father and her body was beginning to scare me. Where did all those titties come from? And the girl's hips and butt were bigger than mine! I thought about myself at sixteen and prayed she wasn't as wild as

I had been.

"Wear 'em up," I finally told her. "It almost makes you look *grown and sexy*." I got up and strutted around.

"Mama, I'm sixteen now. I *am* grown and *sexy*."

"*Mmm hmm*." I waved my hand.

"Can you help me after I get my clothes on?" I nodded my head and before she turned to leave she yelled, "It looks real good downstairs Daddy!"

"Thanks babe!" Aaron yelled from the shower.

Four hours later the first floor was packed with teenagers blasting music and Aaron and I were trying to block it out. Every now and then, Aaron would tip toe downstairs just to remind the kids that there were adults in the house. JaLea had begged us not to embarrass her by trying to dance and fit in. So there we were, laying in our bed, reminiscing about Jalea's first steps and birthdays, her first day of school and how I'd cried because she was scared. Then Aaron dropped a bomb on me.

"I got laid off.' The statement cut like a knife through my thoughts. I did a couple of quick calculations of the savings and bank accounts in my head and groaned at the ridiculous amount we'd spent on JaLea's birthday. The money I made as a party planner couldn't keep up the lifestyle we'd become accustomed to with two incomes. The mortgage, car notes, homeowner's and car insurance was almost my monthly income itself. On top of that, there were six credit cards, student loans, food, gas, electric, cell phones, JaLea, miscellaneous crap we needed during the month... I felt sick. I could network more and try to double my parties. Maybe I could jack up my prices. Maybe I could...

"Kyra?" Aaron's voice sliced into my train of thought again. "They been cutting people left and right all month but remember I said they told me my spot was safe. I gave them ten years. *Ten damn years*!" I was racking my brain. Maybe Tasha wouldn't mind helping us a little. "Kyra, say something." My mouth went dry and I was speechless. I wanted to tell him we'd figure something out, that I loved him and it wasn't his fault. But nothing would come out. Music seeped into my head and I thought once more about JaLea's two-hundred dollar hair and her hundred and fifty dollar outfit. I still had the receipts for her hundred dollar shoes and her eighty dollar chain. No- I couldn't take her gifts back…no, that wouldn't be right.

Aaron got up and left, obviously annoyed by my silence. Yeah, I'd heard about the construction layoff, and those bastards *had* told my husband he was safe. We thought they were telling the truth. How was I supposed to be the bread winner? All those years, my income had just been a little more than cushion. Icing on the cake. A reward for having a hobby I could actually get paid for. Aaron's wages were what kept us afloat.

When Aaron got back to the bedroom, he told me everything was alright with the party but I could still see the defeat on his face. The thought that soon he wouldn't be able to take care of his family was killing him. I pulled him down on the bed and tugged his shirt off to rub his back. His muscles were so tight I was getting excited. He turned to lay me down and I told myself we could talk about our little situation later. As soon as his hand started up my shirt, we heard screams coming from downstairs.

Aaron was way ahead of me, pulling his t-shirt over his head and taking the steps two at a time. By the time I fought through the sea of teenagers, Aaron was on the floor of the den shaking an unconscious girl to death.

"Aaron!" I yelled at him. Whatever was wrong, shaking the hell out of her wasn't helping anything. I stooped down in her face trying to ignore the cries around me. JaLea, horrified, clung to her father's waist as I studied the young girl's face. She was clammy and wet with sweat. Her eyes were barely open and her hair and clothes stuck to her. Her breathing was shallow and raspy. "Call the police!" I yelled.

***

The young girl, Shandi Bradshaw, put a huge rift in my family's life. Apparently, she had Ecstasy in her system and got herself all worked up to the point that she just passed out. A fifteen year old almost overdosed in my house at a rowdy party and not one kid knew the truth about when, where or how she got the drugs. The heat fell on Aaron and me- hard. Every aspect of our lives was scrutinized from where we got our money to what kind of grades JaLea made. The fact that Aaron had just gotten laid off did sit *not* well with the investigators or family services. They were determined to find an underlying reason why he wasn't working. Never mind the fact that the company had been downsizing before the incident even occurred.

About a month later, the investigation was abandoned because there wasn't any sufficient evidence to take any action against us. Shandi Bradshaw was alive and well and the humiliation had died down at JaLea's school. Aaron's last check had come and there had been way more than enough to pay April's bills. Even so, Aaron's depression was becoming more and more apparent. I'd tried reassuring him that we'd be okay, but without having found a job, he didn't know what to do with himself.

JaLea and I had just made it home from visiting Mama one weekend and I called for Aaron but he didn't answer. Once I made it to the bedroom, I saw the bathroom was closed. I called out to him and he kinda grunted. "I thought I told you not to stink up my bathroom!" I laughed, turned on the television, got settled, and waited for him to come out. After twenty minutes, I got antsy and knocked. Five minutes later I knocked again and when no answer followed the second knock, I panicked. I closed and locked the bedroom door, just in case JaLea felt like being nosy, and slowly eased into the bathroom, afraid of what I might find. There was my husband, wedged between the toilet and the tub with his head hanging and a needle sticking out of his arm.

TWENTY-TWO

"How long?" After the hysteria had passed and I knew Aaron would be alright, anger set in. I'd already dropped JaLea off at Mama's on the way to the hospital and called to let them both know he was in the clear. I stood over his bed clenching my purse to keep from smothering him with his pillow. My mind flashed back to the scene at the house, back to JaLea pounding on the door after hearing my screams. It took all the energy and strength left in me to drag her, kicking and screaming, back to her room and pin her to the bed after calling the police. Aaron may have disgraced himself before me and God, but I refused to let his daughter see him like that. No matter how much she fought and begged me.

"I'm sorry," he finally answered, sounding pitiful.

"How long, Aaron?"

"I just been in so much pain."

"What about my pain? What about your daughter's pain!" I didn't even have the tears left to cry. "So is this why you were so-called *laid off* when we thought your position was safe?"

"No!" he yelled defensively. "It's only been going on for two weeks."

"Why Aaron?"

"I been frustrated baby. I can't take care of my own family."

"And you think shootin' that shit in your arm was

helping you take care of your family? You couldn't talk to me? I'm your wife. What am I here for if you can't even talk to me?"

"I'm sorry. I don't know what else to say."

"Say it's over. Say you scared the hell out of yourself and your family enough to stop."

He huffed and squeezed his eyes tight. "Did JaLea see me?" he asked.

"Do you care?" He tried to roll his eyes but it didn't work. "I mean, closing the bathroom door? Ooh, you really tried to hide it from her, didn't you?"

"Kyra, I don't need this right now."

"You need somebody to go off on you and tell you how stupid and selfish this is. Your mama is happy you're okay but she won't even come to see you she's so disappointed. You thought about *your*self and *your* pain. What about us? What if they hadn't been able to save your ass in the ambulance? Our lives would've been much worse than your bruised ego." My heart pounded out of my chest and I couldn't believe I was having that conversation with him.

"I know you're mad…"

"Mad doesn't begin to cover it."

"Honestly, I just needed something to take my mind off everything. A friend of mine offered me some stuff…"

"A *friend* of yours? A friend wouldn't put you in this situation. Where is your friend now? This ain't high school and we ain't teenagers no more. We are grown and our *friends* don't pressure us into taking drugs!" I was out of breath and Aaron's tears rolled into his ears. I wanted to feel sorry for him but he'd brought this all on himself. Plus, he'd dug himself into an even bigger hole. He thought he couldn't find a job before. Who did he think would hire him with drugs in his system?

"I don't know what to say, baby. I know you're disappointed in me and I can't say anything but I'm sorry." He reached for my hand and my first instinct was to pull away, but I let him hold it until a knock at the door interrupted us.

"Hey," Tasha stuck her head in the door. Among all the confusion, I hadn't even remembered calling her. After she exchanged kind words with Aaron, we both stepped out. "How is he?" she asked once we were seated and the door was closed.

"Physically, he's okay for now. He had way more than his body could handle in such a short time. I just can't understand what's goin' on in his head. He claims he started doin' it because he couldn't find a job and was stressed out."

"You think you know somebody." Tasha shook her head. "I never would've pegged him to be the type to do something like this." She only stayed a few more minutes. She had just wanted to make sure I was okay before she stopped to see JaLea at my mama's. She was trying her best to cheer me up and I was acting like it was working but I think she knew I was just playing the part. After a while, we hugged and she wished me well and left. Aaron wanted me to stay, but I knew JaLea needed me. Maybe deep down I needed her more.

***

Aaron's homecoming wasn't what he expected. After a week in the hospital, I arrived, alone, to pick him up. Granted, it had only been a week, but JaLea had lost all respect for her father.

"Where's my baby?" he asked when he got in the car. I already had my lie ready.

"She stayed home to study. She has a big test coming up." The truth was she hadn't wanted to ride with me. She hadn't even wanted to be home when he got there but I told her not to be *so* stubborn. After she got over the shock of her father being in the hospital, reality set in. He was there because he was on drugs.

"How could he be so stupid?" she'd asked. I started to tell her to watch her mouth. Instead, I let her vent. I figured it was better for her to talk to me about it than to any of her lil' fast, big-mouthed friends. "Why would he do that? Why would he leave us?" I didn't know what to tell her. I was just as disappointed as she was, if not more.

"I guess it was hard for her to see me in the hospital." Aaron said matter-of-factly. He sounded bothered that she didn't visit him. I almost laughed. Why would he even want her to see him like that?

Music blasted from upstairs when we finally made it home.

"JaLea! I'm back!" Aaron yelled over the radio. "JaLea!" he repeated before heading up to her room. She was laying face down on her bed, tapping her feet to the tune. "Hey babe, daddy's home." She didn't budge, so Aaron cut the power to the radio. "JaLea, I'm home"

"I heard you," she muttered, turning over.

"Then you better get over here and give me a hug." JaLea got up, but, instead of hugging her father, she walked right past him and down the stairs. "What the hell is her problem?" He was more pissed than hurt and was on his way out the door before I stopped him.

"She's upset, Aaron. You put this family through a lot."

"You told her everything!?" He had an attitude and his six foot, two inch frame towered over me but I wasn't about to bite my tongue. Nobody was going to act like he hadn't been hospitalized for a week because of a drug overdose, no matter how much he wanted us to.

"Your daughter is sixteen years old Aaron. She's not blind and she's not stupid! What was I supposed to tell her, that Daddy had to take a little vacation?"

"Don't play games with me Kyra."

"I'm serious as hell and if you don't realize that, then that's really sad."

"Excuse me," JaLea cut in. Up until then, I hadn't paid attention to the fact that we were still in her room. Aaron walked out first, acting like she wasn't even standing there, and, on my way out, JaLea handed me the mail. My blood was boiling and I wanted to get a lot off my chest but, flipping through the envelopes, my heart stopped. *Bill, junk, junk, bill, and a letter from the Downtown St. Louis Prison Parole Board.* My hands shook and I couldn't get the envelope open fast enough. I could've screamed to the top of my lungs but instead I just read the letter over and over again in disbelief.

After sixteen years, Theresa was getting out of prison.

TWENTY-THREE

Over the years, I'd made it to four of Theresa's five parole hearings. A recent client of mine had demanded so much of my time that I hadn't been able to make it to the last one, and now Theresa would be out in three months. Four times I'd pleaded my case and relived the most horrific three hours of my life. My testimony helped, but it was by Theresa's own fault that she'd been locked up nine years longer than her original sentence.

She'd been in fights, assaulted guards, smuggled drugs, and been denied parole each time she was given a chance. I couldn't help thinking that if I'd shown up to the last parole hearing then she'd be locked up another couple of years at least. I had to sit down and think. Theresa would be a free woman on August third. What would her mindset be? Would she still want revenge? No doubt she blamed me for her having to spend half her life in prison, but they wouldn't release her if she wasn't stable... would they?

"Mama," JaLea interrupted my thoughts. "Why is the mail all over the floor?" I thought about sitting her down and discussing with her the secret that was as old as she was. Aaron and I had always said we'd talk to her about her kidnapping when she was old enough, just so she wouldn't hear it from someone else. I decided it wasn't the right time. She had enough on her mind with her father just getting home.

"I didn't feel like bending over to pick 'em up. I tried my

best to keep my voice steady. She squinted her eyes and I knew she didn't believe me, but she picked the mail up anyway.

"Mama," I heard the unsure tone in her voice and knew what was coming. "Do you think I was wrong?"

"For what, being upset with your daddy?" She nodded.

"I really don't know what to say to him. I mean… it's embarrassing. It really is."

"I know baby." I grabbed her hand and pulled her down on my lap. She was sixteen, but she was still my baby.

***

The weeks flew by but the tension eased slowly. Aaron and JaLea were on talking terms but Aaron and I were barely speaking. We'd only had sex twice and I was horny as hell. I was so horny seeing people kissing on television pissed me off. I was confused because looking at him both aroused and disappointed me at the same time. My husband used to be thick with sexy ripples covering his abdomen. After a week of hospital food he'd slimmed down a little, but, since he'd been home, he had continued to lose weight. I didn't want to believe he was still using drugs, but I couldn't think of any other explanation. I was dying to ask but there was no use. He'd only lie. He walked past just then and I felt a pain in my chest. Aaron was swimming in a tank top that used to hug his chest so tight I could see his nipples. His shorts hung off a little too but I still wanted to straddle him on the couch.

"Hey babe." His voice was low and dry and it turned me off. He was on his way upstairs and I couldn't help thinking how ridiculously pitiful he looked. Not the type of pitiful that deserved sympathy, the type that deserved an ass whoopin'. I wanted to rewind the clock back three months, before my husband lost his job, before my family was scrutinized by the Division of Family Services, before Aaron got so depressed he turned to drugs, before I decided party planning was more important than keeping my daughter's kidnapper in prison…

The ringing of the doorbell snapped me back into reality. Aaron had already trudged upstairs so I got up to answer the door. When I looked out the peephole I almost turned back around. Standing on the porch was Shandi Bradshaw, the lil' nappy-head heffa who tried to O.D. on my den floor. I opened the door, wondering what she could possibly want.

"Hi Mrs. Washington. You probably don't remember me…"

"Oh I remember you." How could I forget? She let the investigation by the D.F.S. go on much longer than it should have because she was scared to get in trouble. She knew damn well she brought that mess in my house but she lied and said she got it at the party.

"I wanted to come and apologize." It was that simple to her. It had been two and a half months and I couldn't help but wonder if her mother had finally let the truth about her daughter settle in and decided to send the girl over to apologize for the both of them.

The mother had given us hell. According to her, JaLea needed to be in special education. According to her, Aaron was a homosexual who slept his way to the head of the construction chain. According to her, I wasn't really a party planner. I was a prostitute, and we were passing out Ecstasy as a party favor. When D.F.S. asked her why Shandi was allowed to come to the party in the first place, she said the girl's father gave her permission behind her back and didn't realize the danger he was supposedly putting their daughter in. She claimed had she known she would've forbid it. The woman had covered all her bases and, at that time, I wanted to catch her outside her job and stomp her. I could laugh at myself now and think about how crazy she must've sounded to them. And Shandi went along with the charade.

"I lied to my mama, I lied to the police, I lied to everybody. JaLea hates me, everybody been talkin' about me, and I'm sorry." She looked at me with Precious Moments eyes and I guess she expected me to feel something, but I didn't. I could've cared less if people were talking about her, which seemed to be the only thing that got her choked up. "Is JaLea here?" I started to tell her no but I changed my mind and moved aside to let her in. That's when I heard the gunfire.

I dropped to the floor and, out of the corner of my eye, saw Shandi fall to ground too. I tried to peek around her to see the car but it was already speeding up the street. All I could tell was that it was black and needed a paint job and a good wax. I waited until the car was completely out of sight before I crawled, terrified, over to Shandi. I could hear my heavy breathing over JaLea's screams which were getting closer. Aaron's feet stumbled down the steps but I subconsciously drowned them out when I saw the small, red stream flowing slowly.

I slid back across the carpet and squeezed my eyes shut to keep the room from spinning. My daughter and husband were talking to me. I know they were, but all I could hear was, *"You- killed- me..."* The voice that had haunted me so long ago had returned and was booming through the entire house, repeating itself over and over again. Everywhere I turned I smelled death and it gave me an instant headache. Blood began pouring from the ceiling and all I could do was scream before I passed out.

I came to with my nose burning from the ammonia pack underneath it. The front yard and the living room were crawling with police and detectives. *Damn* I thought to myself. How long had I been out? I felt like I was in a real life episode of CSI.

"Shandi..." I mumbled, remembering why I'd passed out in the first place.

"She was hit in the shoulder. She'll be fine." Aaron was behind the paramedic who was checking my vitals. JaLea clung to his arm. It occurred to me that we were going to have to deal with Shandi's mother who'd more than likely want the police to stake out my house.

Hours of questioning passed before we had the house to ourselves. I'd wanted to go to the hospital to see Shandi, but I knew I wouldn't be welcome. JaLea was worn out and headed up to bed. Aaron looked like he'd aged five years, pacing the living room, and rubbing his hands through back and forth over waves. He looked so tired and worn, but, before I could reach out to him, he headed towards the kitchen. When he was out of my line of sight, the phone rang. He didn't let it get through a full ring before he picked up.

God gave women a sixth sense and mine told me to sneak on the line.

"Uh, ye- yeah, the police are gone," Aaron stuttered.

"Good," a deep voice answered. "If I'd been aiming, it would've been your wife's head." It took everything in me not to scream. "I want my money and I'm not fuckin' playin. Next time I'm snatchin' that sexy lil' daughter of yours."

TWENTY-FOUR

I was living in a nightmare. My legs felt like tree trunks on my way to the kitchen. And there was Aaron sitting at the table looking moronic as ever.

"Who was on the phone?" He perked up at the sound of my voice.

"Oh that was a wrong number. I'm just thinking about that little girl." It wasn't until then that reality finally hit me like a bolt of lightning. It shot through me so fast I didn't know what happened until my hand was numb and Aaron was grabbing his face.

"What the hell…"

"*You* are the reason that child is laying up in the hospital!" I yelled.

"I don't know what you're talking about." He tried to get up and I slapped him again.

"You gone stop putting yo hands on me! What the hell is yo problem?"

"*My* problem? Are you serious?!" The storm inside me was uncontrollable a that point. "*You* are my problem, Aaron. In case you haven't guessed by now, I overheard your little conversation. Wrong number my *ass*!"

"Baby…" he reached out to me and I jerked away. "I'm taking care of it."

"How much do you owe?" I wanted to know but I didn't. I could come up with money if it meant saving JaLea, but I didn't want Aaron to think I was doing it for him.

"I told you I'm taking care of it." There was that ego.

"You *have* been getting money from somewhere haven't you? I can't keep up with the bills by myself, our cable and cell phones are off, Chrysler gone come in a hot minute to repossess your car 'cause you know I'm not letting *my* ride go. My credit is going down the drain because I can barely pay the minimum due, yet *you* get money from somewhere to keep doing the shit you're doing instead of helping with business at home. But apparently you can't keep up either. How much do you owe Aaron?" He looked dead into my eyes and I knew he was debating on whether or not to lie.

"A thousand dollars, but I'm taking care of it."

"A thousand dollars! Where in the hell are you planning to get a thousand dollars? Who do you think you are, Wesley Snipes in *New Jack City*? This is not a movie. It's not a *game*! Jalea's life is in danger!" My hands were shaking and I felt the urge to slap him again, but he caught my arm in the air and spun me around, pulling my back against his chest.

"Calm down baby, please. Let's sit down and talk about this." I tried to wiggle free but it was no use.

"What is there to talk about? You racked up a thousand dollars worth of debt with a man who wants to shoot me in the head and rape your daughter if you don't pay him back. How are you *taking care of it*?" He let me go and I turned to look at him. "You wanted to talk so tell me. How are you planning on taking care of it?" He was stumped. Looking at him with that stupid, lost look on his face made me want to pack my daughter up and leave. "You think about that," I told him. "JaLea and I will be at Mama's."

"They know where she stays." Without thinking, I picked up the phone and dialed her number.

"Hey Mama."

"Kyra? What's wrong? What time is it?" I heard the

125

panic in her voice and immediately regretted calling.

"It's almost eleven, Mama. I didn't know it was this late. Go back to sleep." I got off and glared at Aaron. "I'll go to Tasha's…"

"They know where she stays too."

"Well damnit Aaron, why don't *you* leave?" I couldn't believe how good it felt to tell him that. He'd been a hindrance since he got home from the hospital. How much more of a burden could he possibly be?

"What happened to 'for better or worse'?"

"Don't try to run that shit on me. I'm not asking for a divorce. I'm telling you I don't wanna look at your face and I want you the hell outta my house."

"*Your* house?!"

"Yes, *my* house. I been bustin' my ass the past three months payin' the mortgage…"

"Bustin' yo ass?"

"Yes, bustin' my ass!"

"Doin' what, decoratin'? Let me see you lay some foundation then you can say you been bustin' yo ass."

"When was the last time you laid some foundation? Only thing you been bustin' yo ass for is that shit that had you laid up in the hospital! It sure as hell ain't been for this family, I know that much! You're sickening! Look at yourself, you can't even fit your clothes! You look disgusting and I don't want you anywhere near me or JaLea. Go to Marcus's house or something. Please."

"Marcus is the one that got me into this."

"How did Marcus get you into this?"

"He's the one that hooked me up, showed me where to get it. A lot of times he gives me money to get it." I laughed. Not because it was funny, but because I was just taken back. Other that the drunken run-in I'd had with Aaron's uncle years earlier, he'd proven to be decent. He was family. He'd been in my house, spent time with my daughter, my mother…and all the while he was helping ruin my family. My delirious laughter turned into heaving, uncontrollable sobs.

"Baby calm down." He tried to grab my arm.

"Get the hell off me!" I shoved his hands away. "How am I supposed to calm down, huh? My husband is a crack head who can't find a job and has his dealers shootin' up my house. I'm gonna loose my car, probably the house because I won't be able to get any clients after Shandi's mama finishes running her mouth. Theresa will be out in a month…"

"Theresa! When did that happen?"

"It doesn't matter. There's nothing we can do about it now. But what you can do for me is leave. You and your crack pushin' uncle can kiss my ass! Tell him to help you come up with the thousand dollars with his old ass." I turned to leave the kitchen but kept talking. "Almost fifty and sellin'. He need to be ashamed. Yeah, have him help you *take care of it*. Just make sure you stay away from me and JaLea."

"That's not fair babe." He was on my heels, following me through the hall. I had to turn and stop him short.

"*Not fair*! What's not fair is the fact that you got me and JaLea mixed up in *yo* mess. I swear if my child gets hurt…" Fear started digging a hole into my heart. I couldn't fathom the thought of anyone getting their hands on JaLea.

"I won't let anybody hurt her."

"Aaron you don't have control over those people. This is not the time to listen to your ego. They know everything about us and, let you tell it, our family and friends too. You can't b.s. these people. You need to figure out what you're gonna do to get out of this and you need to do it away from me and my daughter."

TWENTY-FIVE

Two weeks passed before I heard from Aaron again and I had begun to worry. I'd explained the situation in part to JaLea. All she needed to know was that her father needed to work on his problems and he needed to do that elsewhere. She answered the phone when he called and had no conversation for him; she just passed the phone to me.

I was already in a bad mood because, as I predicted, Shandi's mother had been working her mouth. At first I had no idea what she was saying, but when my current client fired me abruptly and demanded a refund for her deposit, I knew something was up. I'd spent the past four days marketing, trying to make up for what I'd lost. Tasha had been using her radio influence to find out if I was just being paranoid. Sure enough, Shandi's mother had gone to great lengths to defame me. Only this time, her information was factual. My crack head husband had gotten her daughter shot. So at that moment, Aaron's was the last voice I wanted to hear.

"Hey babe."

"Hey."

"I guess you told JaLea why I left. She doesn't really wanna talk to me." I tried to listen to his voice and see if he was high or not, but I couldn't tell.

"Not everything. Some details she just doesn't need." Some details she probably heard from nosy, jabber-mouth classmates.

"How's everything going?"

"Fine. What's up?" I was tired of the small talk. It had been two whole weeks and I wanted to know what he wanted. If he wasn't calling to say he was clean then I didn't wanna hear it. He couldn't possibly have been calling to see how we were.

"Nobody's called there for me have they?"

"What is it Aaron?"

"Here's the thing babe. I got about half of the money but I need a little help."

"I told you I can't help you."

"Can't you sell the car?"

"*My* car? No. See, *your* car got repossessed and I'm definitely not selling mine. And if I decide to in the future it won't be for you, it'll be to catch up on all the bills I'm behind on.

"Why don't you call Tasha?"

"Tasha does not have money like that to give away. Are you high Aaron? You still finding a way to shoot up even though you owe them money? Even though your wife is struggling trying to keep her head above water."

"Baby I know you could get a good two thousand for the car if not more." I hung up on him. He deserved it. He was high and didn't hear a word that had come out of my mouth.

"Mama, what did Daddy want?" JaLea asked.

"Nothing," I lied.

"When the phone rang at almost midnight, I figured it was him again, but it wasn't.

"Kyra, this is Marcus."

"What do you want?" I asked irritated, wiping sleep from my eyes.

"Aaron is in trouble."

"So. What else is new?"

"You can really be a cold hearted bitch, you know that?"

"Thank you."

"Anyway," he sounded annoyed. "Like I said, your man is in trouble. I came home and stuff was everywhere. My place is a mess and Aaron is gone."

"If I'm not mistaken, *you* helped him into this, so what do you expect me to do?"

"You can try to help me think of what to do next."

"Marcus I don't even really know what ya'll are into. I don't know those people that are lookin' for him. *You* do. I don't know where they live, where they hang out, or where they'd take Aaron. *You* do. What I *do* know is how far they'll go to get their money and I do *not* want any part of that."

"So you're just gonna give up on him? Just like that?"

"If you must be all up in my business, I'm not giving up on him. I'm giving him a chance to straighten himself out before he comes back home. If he can't straighten out, then that's on him. All that that he's into, I don't need it and JaLea definitely doesn't need to be around it."

"But how can I find him?"

"Are you listening to me or are you high right now too? I told you I have no idea what to do." I heard a click and held the phone to my ear until I heard the operator. By that time, my sheet was wet from tears. No matter how much I tried to make myself believe I didn't care, I was dying inside. I'd tried to be as nonchalant as possible with Marcus, but I knew what I felt in my heart. I wanted to do whatever I could to help Aaron get that money. I had devoted more than half my life to him and we'd been through hell and back. If I wasn't trying to be so stubborn, I probably would've sold my car. But I was scared to fit into that stereotype of the stupid woman working her ass off to take care of her no good man. I deserved better than what Aaron was giving me and I knew he was capable of it. He'd hit a rough patch. Damn a rough patch, he'd hit rock bottom, and he needed me. Besides, that money would help keep me and JaLea out of harm's way. I didn't have to give in completely. I just needed to find a way to come up with some money fast. I called back but there was no answer at Marcus's house.

After two weeks had passed, I still hadn't been able to get in touch with Marcus or Aaron. I hadn't been able to find work or come up with any money either. I hid my worry from JaLea who I figured was oblivious to the seriousness of situation. I poured my heart out to Mama though. Even though she was fuming, she understood my plight. She didn't offer any insight though.

"That's one you're gonna have to figure out for yourself. Helping him could either save or ruin your marriage. So could doing nothing." she told me. I felt no better having talked to Mama and I was still worried sick about my husband.

It was pitch black out by the time I picked JaLea up from a friend's house. I decided to park in the back instead of on the street because I'd become slightly paranoid on the way home. JaLea had sensed it.

"You okay, Mama?" she asked once we got out. Then her eyes widened in horror as a ghastly noise fought to escape her lips. Before I could turn towards the object of her dismay, two massive arms caught hold of me.

"Don't fight…" The husky voice immediately struck me as the voice of the man who had called the house the day of the drive-by. Knowing the things this man had said made me more scared than I'd ever been in my life. My stomach did acrobatic flips at the thought of JaLea having to endure the torture of rape. I was surprised I could keep myself from wetting my pants. The man put a knife to my throat and my legs became noodles. He grabbed me around my waist and that was the only reason I didn't fall to the ground. I tried to tell JaLea to run but the tip of the knife piercing the side of my neck was stopping the words before they hit my lips.

"Be quiet. And you," he nodded toward JaLea. "You

stay your sexy ass right there." I wished JaLea had been thinking the way I was. The man had a knife in one hand and was holding me with the other. I was almost certain she could outrun him. I was also almost certain he had a gun. If she took off running, he'd probably loosen his grip, simply from seeing her getting away. Then maybe I could get to my mace. But JaLea didn't run. She was frozen in place, watching the tip of the knife slowly and excruciatingly piercing the side of my neck.

"Your husband owes me two thousand dollars." *Didn't Aaron say he owed him one thousand?* "That means *you* owe me two thousand dollars. I'm tired of playing with ya'll asses. Yo' man thought he was too good and got hisself fucked. Now he's into me for two g's. I don't like games when it come to my money." My heart rate had sped up and I could feel blood trickling down my neck but I refused to scare my daughter by screaming out in agony. She was staying put like he told her. "You got a week," he hissed in my ear. When he let go, I toppled to the ground and he ran off. I wanted to turn and look at him but my body was weak from fear.

JaLea stooped down to help me up and I felt light-headed as I stood to my feet. The blood from my wound had seeped into the collar of my shirt. I took one look at my daughter's panic-stricken face and my pain was replaced with malice. My hands shook from the undeniable urge to whoop Aaron's crack head ass.

TWENTY-SIX

I had too much on my mind the next day. I practically had to pry myself away from JaLea to leave the house. I didn't feel like driving all over St. Louis looking for my husband, but I would if I had to.

I looked crazy with a big ass band-aid plastered on my neck like a junior high school girl trying to hide a passion mark. I'd brushed my hair a little bit but it still looked like crap. Neither I nor JaLea had gotten any sleep and there I was at the crack of dawn peering on street corners like I was looking for a fix.

I had to find Aaron so we could come up with a way to get this money. He said he had about half of it, but he told me he owed a thousand. The dealer said two thousand. So there was no telling how much money Aaron had, if in fact he had any money at all. What if he hadn't lied to me though? What if Aaron thought he owed a thousand but the dealer had gone up to two thousand? If that was the case, then Aaron only had about five hundred dollars and needed another fifteen hundred. Either way, that man wanted two thousand. On top of that, I hadn't done a party in two months, the checking and saving accounts were dwindling faster than I'd anticipated, and Theresa would be a free woman in a matter of hours.

I thought about calling Tasha, but I knew she couldn't help. I didn't feel like hearing her mouth anyway. I loved her and she was my girl, but she wasn't married and she wouldn't understand. Hell, she didn't even have a *man*! It would've been easy for her to tell me to just leave. And I wouldn't dare ask Mama to dip into her savings. I already knew she was more than pissed at Aaron. She didn't act like a fool about it, but I know my mama. I'd exhaust my possibilities before thinking about asking her.

I stopped at a payphone to call and check on JaLea. I was scared to leave her but didn't want her riding with me. In the end, I decided she would be better off at home, especially if I found Aaron and he was strung out. After I'd checked on her, I pulled into a lot and sat looking at the clock. It was almost noon and I'd been out for hours. Aaron's family probably thought I was losing my mind as many time as I knocked on their doors, and I'd been by Marcus's house five times. I was running on empty and Grey Goose was calling my name. I needed something, anything… MD, Hypnotik, Smirnoff, Vodka… I felt like an alcoholic, I wanted a drink so bad. Instead, I strolled into the dollar store and bought a Strawberry Vess and a 'For Sale' sign I knew I'd eventually have to put in my car window.

Sitting there drinking my soda gave me time to think over my life. I used to think I was so lucky. I had a smart, beautiful daughter, a sexy, hardworking husband who loved the hell outta me, a glamorous house and a job I loved. Now my world was in shambles. If Aaron hadn't gotten laid off, would Marcus have been able to talk him into that mess? Was Marcus doing drugs too?

I looked in my rearview mirror and said aloud, "Your husband is a crack head and you're about to sell your car to keep his dealer happy." Hearing the words coming out of my mouth made me wonder how we could ever get past it. I used to cherish Aaron. I thought he was the best thing that had ever happened to me, besides JaLea. I thanked God that I hadn't found the means to get an abortion, but I couldn't help letting my mind wander. If

Aaron hadn't been the father, then what? Where would I have been in life? Where would my daughter be? One thing I was certain of, I wouldn't be broke and sitting in the parking lot of a dollar store daydreaming and trying to figure out how to pay off a drug dealer before my family ended up on the Channel 2 News.

It was 1:20 p.m. Theresa had officially been a free woman for an hour and twenty minutes, I wanted to call her mother, whom I hadn't spoken to since the day Theresa took JaLea. I didn't even know if they'd spoken much, but I was curious. Who'd picked Theresa up? Where was she staying? Who was she with? Was she still crazy as hell? Had she realized how wrong she was? It became a bizarre obsession as I pulled off the lot. I wanted to find Theresa as much as I needed to find Aaron but I didn't know where to look for either.

Ten minutes later I pulled into Marcus's driveway again, not expecting to find Aaron there at all, but there was a car there. I hurt myself trying to rush to the front door. Music blasted and I wondered if they were in there getting high and shooting up more money while I was racking my brain trying to come up with ways to pay back what Aaron already owed.

I pounded on the door but there was no answer. I jogged around back, unable to contain myself, and pounded on that door too. It creaked open and the music hit me, along with the disgusting stench of weed. It was hot as hell and I called for Aaron but I couldn't hear my own voice over the music. I became increasingly terrified the deeper I went into the house. Something wasn't right. I could feel it, and, as I pushed open one of the bedroom doors, I was overcome with nausea. There was Aaron's naked, sweaty body rolling around with Theresa.

Deja' gotdamn vu.

TWENTY-SEVEN

I had a flashback of the first night I had caught them together and I was livid. My mind raced with a mixture of confusion and pure rage. The closest thing to me was a video tape on the floor near my foot. I thought about throwing it but picked it up and charged the bed instead. I swung, first hitting Aaron in the back of the head. He rolled over moaning in pain and I hit a wide-eyed Theresa square in the nose, then again in the shoulder when she tried to move away. The only thing that stopped me was a shadow out of the corner of my eye. Marcus was naked too with a camera in his hands videotaping the whole thing and laughing his ass off. My mind would have to comprehend that after I'd finished what I started.

Theresa cowered in a corner where I couldn't get to her so I threw the tape, hitting her in the abdomen. Aaron was walking towards me with his hands out, eyes glazed over. I couldn't tell if his nose was running or if he was sweating just that hard. His shoulder was twitching like he was having a mini seizure. Seeing him like that hurt more than catching him with Theresa… again. He was talking but Eminem blasting through the stereo was drowning him out.

Brain damage, Ever since the day I was born,
Drugs is what they used to say I was on.

They say I never knew which way I was goin'
But everywhere they go they keep playin' my song.
Brain damage.

How gotdamn ironic? I didn't care what Aaron had to say anyway, my blood was boiling. I grabbed a picture from off the television and flung it, catching Aaron's forehead, and he stumbled back. The blood trickling from the gash the frame left only pumped me up more. Taking advantage of his disorientation, I pushed him back on the bed and climbed on top of him.

    The punches came naturally like I was fighting some random person. Aaron was so out of it he didn't try to fight back. I didn't care that my knuckles were numb by the time Marcus finally pulled me off of him. When he let me go, I yanked the radio cord out of the socket. I couldn't hear my own thoughts. Then I remembered that Marcus was naked too. He stood there, scrawny and limp, his bulging eyes unconsciously scanning the room. Clothes and trash littered the floor and, either Marcus was actually telling the truth about someone ransacking his house, or that was just how he lived. I was seriously leaning towards the latter. Aaron had rolled up into a fetal position and Theresa was crouching on the floor twirling her hair. They looked a hot, funky mess. Just for the hell of it, I picked up another picture frame and threw it at Theresa. She tried to block it but it hit her chin anyway and she whimpered.

    "Kyra," Aaron was getting up. "I miss you. Can I come home?" My jaw dropped to the floor. I'd never been face to face with a crack head and I was seeing first hand what four months had done to a perfect human being. He hadn't even wiped the blood from his face. I wondered if this was an everyday thing. Smoke weed, shoot up, have orgies, make pornos, listen to ridiculously loud music… I wondered if he even knew who he was having sex with or if he'd had sex with other women on a daily basis. Damn that! How was he having sex with Theresa not two hours after she was released from prison? He wouldn't have kept in touch with her all these years after the kidnapping, and I'd just assumed Marcus hadn't had anything to do with her.

"Baby..." *Was he still talking?* I needed air. I was getting a damn contact. I tried leaving the three of them to their private party but Aaron grabbed my arm. "I *need* you."

"You didn't need me five minutes ago when you were fuckin the woman who kidnapped your daughter." He looked back at Theresa who was inspecting her toenails. Why was I even still there wasting my time? On my way out, I snatched the camera from Marcus, who was stumbling around aimlessly, and hurled it at the wall, breaking off large pieces. Aaron was following me to the door... dangling... I had to stop him.

"Please, stay right there." I told him. He looked at me like a lost, helpless puppy. I wanted to see in him the man, or even the boy, I'd fell in love with, but there was nothing left. All I could feel for him was pity. I really hoped he could find himself, but I didn't want to sit around waiting. It had taken him four months to ruin what we'd worked seventeen years for. I was embarrassed for him, standing there, naked, in tube socks, merely a portion of the man he once was. There was no broadness in his shoulders, no thickness to his thighs, no pecks on his chest, and no six pack. I needed to get away from there before my pride crumbled and I cried all over the place.

I must've done fifteen miles all the way home. I had to pull over twice to compose myself and wipe the endless flow of tears. Slowly but surely, it was sinking in that my marriage was over. There was no going back. Aaron had done things that were irreparable, unforgivable, disrespectful, and downright immoral. My heart was breaking, shattering into a million pieces that were slamming against my rib cage, and I couldn't take the pain. When I pulled in front of my house all I wanted to do was roll up in the back seat and cry. I couldn't let JaLea see me like that, but, for the life of me, I couldn't make it stop. I pounded on the dashboard, on the steering wheel, on my head... In my own world, my husband was dead. His addiction had taken him away from his family and he was never coming back. But somewhere in the back of my mind, I still wanted answers. Simply knowing what had happened wasn't enough for me. I needed to know *why*. I needed specifics. They'd probably only hurt me more but I couldn't digest the fact that my marriage was over without having all the details. At that moment though, I needed to pull it together, for myself and for JaLea.

She ran to me when I opened the door and I hugged her tight. She went back upstairs without asking any questions and I was thankful for that. I couldn't pretend what I'd seen hadn't happened, that I hadn't caught my husband naked with both a woman *and* a man, or that I'd fought him until my hands went numb. Was he that far gone that he'd been sexual with Marcus too?! I shook the repulsive image from my mind as I pulled bills from a kitchen drawer and my checkbook from my purse.

I had to ask myself why I calculated and recalculated the bills so much? It wasn't like I had a massive fortune to work with. Everything was either due or past due. The only choice I had was to pay *on* this or pay *on* that. I'd already emptied the savings account, and there was only two-fifty left in the joint account. I also had my own account but the five hundred dollars in it may as well have been Monopoly money when it came to the bills. After adding in late and overdraft fees, all I could do was shake my head. I added another two thousand for the pusher because I knew from what I'd witnessed earlier that I couldn't count on Aaron's claims of having half the money. How the hell do you get two thousand dollars worth of crack debt anyway?

The internet was calling my name. I wanted to find out how much I could sell my car for. Before I could get through the initial sign on, a thought occurred to me. If Aaron never got himself together, which seemed inevitable, how would I or

JaLea ever be out of harm's way? Theresa's mind obviously wasn't working right. Would I eventually have to deal with her? And simply praying that JaLea never ran into Aaron anywhere wouldn't work. The wheels in my head started turning. I refused to touch the savings Aaron and I had been putting up for JaLea, but I remembered Mama telling me about the C.D. she'd been building up to pass on to me. There had to be $2500 to $3000 in it. Our list of relatives outside St. Louis was extensive so, after a few calls, I'd finalized my decision. The only way to be completely free of Aaron, and preserve my sanity at the same time, would be to get me and my daughter as far away from St. Louis as possible.

TWENTY-EIGHT

Mama cried when I told her I was leaving, but, after I filled her in on everything that had happened, she agreed to close out the C.D. She said it would take a couple of days to get it out and cashed. I had six days before that man would come back to collect his money. I was a workhorse and was certain I could have things taken care of by then.

My first cousin, Annette, stayed in Atlanta in a beautiful house she had built from the ground up. I'd briefly discussed the situation with her. She knew that Aaron had gotten in a little trouble and JaLea and I needed to get away. She pushed for more details than I was ready to give, but eventually, she let it go and agreed to let JaLea and I use her spare bedroom until I got on my feet. According to her, life was easy in Atlanta and it wouldn't take long to get my own place. She had her daughter's high school e-mail me an enrollment form for JaLea to start school later that month. I didn't hesitate to filling it out. Later that day, I finally sat JaLea down and told her we needed to have a woman to woman conversation.

"Mama, I'm grown," she joked. She stopped when she saw my serious expression.

"Your father is in a lot of trouble. He owes people money and they'll do anything to get it, including hurt us." Her expression didn't change. It occurred to me that she knew that already and saw the conversation as anything but woman to woman. "That man that was here the other night thinks I'm able to pay the money but I can't. Your father can't come up with it either and I don't think he'll be getting better any time soon." She nodded, showing no alarm at all. "We're in some serious danger here. We have to leave St. Louis."

"What!? When?" She looked surprised and excited at the same time.

"This week."

"Will I get to say bye to Daddy?"

"No baby, I'm sorry." She was only slightly disturbed.

"Well, will I get to say bye to Grandma or Tasha or anybody?"

"You can say goodbye to Grandma and Tasha but the fewer people that know we're leaving the better. Friends will have to wait." She looked a little defeated.

"I know you think I don't understand but I do. I figured you didn't wanna talk about last night, so I left it alone. I know it was bad enough for us to have to leave. You don't have to tell me, but Mama I do understand." She paused, and then smiled. "So where are we going?"

"Atlanta with Annette and her daughter, Camille. Remember them?"

"Atlanta? The *ATL*! Seriously!"

"Yes, JaLea." I was immensely relieved. I would never have expected that reaction from her. "We can't take much, only what can fit in the Envoy. Pack all your clothes and shoes and anything else has to be very, very important."

"Okay, Mama." She ran upstairs.

"Very important!" I called after her.

I had a lot of running to do that day. After I made a list of things I needed to get done, I stopped at the post office to put in change of address forms. Then, I went to the bank and closed out my accounts. For the checking and savings accounts, I got $762.13. I closed JaLea's savings account and got the $1325 in a check so I could redeposit it once we got to Atlanta. The bank manager tried to talk me into other accounts and investments and I ended up getting an attitude with him when he wouldn't shut up. That lil' bald man was wasting my time and I had things to do.

I wanted to stop at the McDonald's near Tasha's house to see if they had any boxes. Then I planned on breaking the news to her. She just happened to be there getting something to eat.

"Movin'?" she joked when she saw me with the boxes.

"Actually, I am." Her smile faded quickly.

Tasha and I settled into a booth in the very back of the restaurant where I confessed everything I'd been holding back from her. She stayed quiet with a confused look on her face and, when I finally finished, she was crying silently.

"That son-of-a-bitch," she whispered through soft sobs. "Kyra… damn, I wish I had some money or something. I could…"

"I don't want your money, but I *was* on my way to ask you for a favor."

"Anything."

"Sell my furniture and my house."

"Wha- huh? How?" She snapped out of her trance.

"We have to leave this week and I don't have time to do it." I gave her a hundred dollar bill." This is for furniture storage. Don't move anything out of the house until after we get to Atlanta. Anything you don't sell right away you can put in storage to start trying to sell the house. I don't care how you sell the stuff or who you sell it to. You keep half the profit and send the rest to me." I handed her an index card with the Atlanta address on it. "You can use the hundred dollars to run for sale ads in the paper too. After you sell the house send a third of it to Mama and the rest to me." She sat stone faced, soaking everything in. "I know you can do this for me," I reassured her. Then, I handed over the deed to my house.

"It looks like you got everything planned out, but don't you think this is a little extreme. You can't think of anything else?" Her eyes pleaded with me, carrying twenty-three years of friendship and memories.

"Can *you*?" She shook her head and dropped it, looking at the things I'd given her.

"You need any help packing?"

"I'm not packing much, just necessities. You can help clean up some. Whatever you want you can have and I guess you can take Aaron's clothes and shoes to his uncle's house after we leave. If he's not there leave 'em on the porch or take 'em to the Goodwill. I don't really care." I did care but I wasn't about to admit it.

"Well, I guess everything's covered. Damn I wish I had some money to give you."

"It wouldn't matter one way or the other. Aaron's not stopping anytime soon, so what's the point in handing over $2,000? So that whenever he gets in trouble JaLea and I are in the hot seat too? I can't be scared forever. That bastard left us no choice."

"You better say bye to me and let me say bye to my god-daughter."

"You know I will." We hugged and headed our separate ways.

When I pulled up in front of the house, Aaron was sitting on the porch. *Damn*! What the hell did he want?

"Baby!" He ran towards me when I got out but I didn't want anyone to see him.

"Go around back," I told him in a loud whisper. He obediently turned to go through the gangway and into the back yard. He was already sitting on the porch when I rounded the back of the house. The closer I got to him, the harder I had to try to act like I didn't notice how funky he was.

"I miss you," he said.

"That's not what you came here for." I didn't know if he'd knocked on the door or not. JaLea didn't *even* need to know he was around.

"I saw the tape." I started to ask what tape he was talking about, but it quickly came back to me. I guess I'd only damaged the camera when I threw it at the wall. "The things I did... I ... Kyra, I'm sorry." I just stood there glaring at him with my hands on my hips. "You know I hate Theresa. If my mind was right, it wouldn't have even went down like that."

"How did she even get there?" That's when his rambling began.

"I had some money hid for my guy, remember the money I told you I had? Well, I lost it- no- somebody took it. And I looked everywhere. I left 'cause I thought it was Marcus. I slept with friends here and there but I really didn't have nowhere to stay so I went back to Marcus's. He said I could come back if I rode somewhere wit' him so I did. He didn't tell me where we was going baby, I swear I didn't even know that was the day she was gettin' out. I mean, I remember you tellin' me and everything, but I didn't know. She had some stuff from some people and I *had* to try it. You don't understand, I *had* to. When we got back to the house- man- things got out of hand. I think it was laced with somethin'. So you forgive me, right?"

"Are you crazy? You just told me you were so messed up you didn't really know you were having sex with the woman who kidnapped your daughter until you saw it on videotape!"

"I *know*, I know it sound bad right?" He'd started scratching his neck. "I wanna come home." He stood and I backed up, afraid of what he might try to do. "I miss you and my baby..." He looked around the yard, confused. *Did he forget her damn name!*

"JaLea." I reminded him. He nodded and I wanted to smack the hell out of him. How could he forget his own daughter's name? He was scratching uncontrollably at this point and I couldn't stand looking at him anymore. "Aaron, get the hell outta my yard and don't come back." I pointed towards the gangway and he was dumbfounded.

"I didn't forget her name and I'm trying to apologize to you." He took the steps down slowly and I backed further into the yard. "Why won't you listen to me?"

"You are trippin' right now, Aaron. You been trippin' for a long time and the best thing for me and JaLea would be for you to leave." He looked like he was about to rush me but he walked past, reluctantly, staring at me with evil eyes. I watched fearfully, praying that he didn't decide he wanted to see JaLea. He kept going though, staggering a little with every step. There was no telling whether or not Aaron still had his house key but I made a mental note that I'd have to get the locks changed. As far as my marriage was concerned, I'd gotten the closure I needed.

TWENTY-NINE

I got up at 9 a.m. the next morning. With only four days left to come up with the money, I wanted to be gone in three. The first thing I did was call the locksmith. They couldn't come out until the next morning, which was fine as long as they were there between nine and eleven like they said. I called the phone, gas, and electric companies to notify them of the move.

JaLea and I took all the pictures off the walls and gathered up important papers and knick knacks. We stuffed all our purses and filled four suitcases with shoes and clothes, leaving out only what we needed for the next four days. I jumped on the internet with the intent of looking for work in Atlanta, but Annette had already sent me information for two potential clients. A 25th wedding anniversary and a 30th birthday. My creative mind started clicking with ideas as I read through their information. I jotted everything down and left it by the phone to remind myself to call my new clients. Hell, I was already making money.

Later that day, JaLea and I met Mama and Tasha at Applebee's for dinner. We laughed and talked trying to stay away from the real reason we were all out together, the fact that JaLea and I were moving six-hundred miles away. We reminisced even after dessert had been taken away. I got up to use the restroom and a face caught my eye for only a moment. A memory stirred from deep within my past but I quickly shook the thought away. When I got back to the table, Tasha said she had a surprise for me and pulled out a cell phone.

"It's pre-paid with only a thousand minutes, but you

need something driving all that way. It's a three-one-four area code so we can talk without having to use long distance. And I made sure you can get service in Atlanta without roaming," she told me. JaLea snatched it before I could.

"Ooh, Mama! I miss my phone," she squealed, hugging the cell.

"She's so silly. Thank you, girl."

"I'll have my surprise tomorrow," Mama said. "It's more than you think." She winked and squeezed my hand. I grinned, wondering how much the certificate of deposit could possibly be. I had just assumed it was around $2,500. I started to say something before that face caught my eye again. A cold blast from my past chilled me to the bone and I smiled, hard and fake, to hide my fear. I began to stall for time, thinking of anything that could keep us there, but, after four hours, everyone was tired and I was fresh out of ideas.

We said our goodbyes and I nervously scanned the restaurant for the hauntingly familiar face, but it was nowhere in sight. The four of us made plans for breakfast and finally left.

It was almost eleven when JaLea and I got home. We each took a suitcase out and put it in the trunk. I wanted to make sure we were discreet, moving a little at a time. We'd already put a box and one of the suitcases in the trunk before leaving for Applebee's.

The message light was blinking and I decided to wait until JaLea finally headed up to bed. There were four messages and four of the missed calls on the caller I.D. were from Marcus's house. Frustrated, I pushed play.

"Baby, uh, this is Aaron. Were you serious yesterday?" *Beep.*

"Kyra, I wanna talk. Can we talk about this please? Please call me. I'm at Marcus's. You know the number." *Beep.*

"Damnit, Kyra, answer the phone! I know you're there. JaLea! JaLea baby, tell Mommy to pick up the phone… JaLea…

JaLea ... answer the gotdamn phone!" *Beep.*

"Kyra?" The first three messages hadn't surprised me, but Theresa's voice sure did. "I'm so sorry I had to take yo' man... *again.*" Then she started laughing. I had the nerve to get my feelings hurt, but I told myself they deserved each other. Hell, I was young. I could get me a sexy, hardworking man in Atlanta with an accent that could make me wet. I erased the messages and fell asleep on the couch dreaming about my dark, southern prince.

I got JaLea up at nine the next morning to take the last suitcase out and start stripping her room down. I wanted closets, walls and drawers cleaned, carpets vacuumed, floors swept, windows washed, and furniture dusted. JaLea and I would sleep on the couches that night, have breakfast with Mama and Tasha the next morning and leave as soon as possible afterwards.

The locksmith showed up at eleven thirty, right before Tasha, and changed the locks to the front and back doors. When he left, I sent JaLea out with another box and she rode with Tasha to get copies of the new keys. While they were gone, Mama showed up to help.

"Mama, you didn't have to come and help." I told her as we folded sheets.

"No bother. I had to come give you this anyway." She pulled an envelope out of her purse and handed it to me. I opened it and almost fell out. I counted ten one-hundred dollar bills and pulled out a check for $15,025.

"Mama! Where the hell did you get this!"

"Watch your mouth!" I covered my mouth with the biggest check I'd ever seen, embarrassed I'd let the curse word slip. "If you must know, I've been savin' money out of almost every check since the day you were born. I wasn't about to let that dope head dip into what I saved all this time for *you*. So you have to promise me, husband or not, on drugs or not, that you will not let that man back into your life."

"I promise, Mama." I had washed my hands of Aaron Washington. I'd always love him because of JaLea, but a relationship just wasn't in our cards anymore. We both burst into tears and hugged until we realized we still had things to do.

Once Tasha and JaLea got back, things moved along fast. By seven that afternoon, the house was spotless. While I whipped up some fried chicken and french fries, Mama and Tasha went around picking out things they wanted. After we ate, I emptied the refrigerator, freezer, and pantry, letting Mama pick things to take home with her. JaLea and I would stop for snacks on the way to Atlanta. Tasha helped me take the mattress out to the dumpster in the alley behind the house and I could've sworn I heard a noise.

"Did you hear that?" I asked her.

"Yeah. Probably just a squirrel or something." I looked up and down the alley for the longest time until Tasha snapped me out of my trance. "You want me to help with the rest of the trash?"

"Girl, that's what JaLea's for." We laughed but when we got back into the house, JaLea had passed out on the couch. "Its fine," I convinced Tasha. "It's not a lot, I got it." She left me to my few bags of trash. On my way out to the alley with the first two bags, I kept telling myself that all I heard was a squirrel and to hurry up and get back in the house. But before I could get the lid up off the trash can, I heard the rustling again, this time much louder.

"You movin'?" The voice came from behind me causing me to spin around, ripping the side of one of the bags. There was the familiar face from Applebee's, the infamous secret from my past, my cheating, drug-dealing, rapist of an ex-boyfriend, Chris.

150

THIRTY

"Chris! Hey!" That was all I could think to say. I tried to sound calm and happy to see him. I wanted to scream bloody murder but I noticed his hands shoved into his pockets. No telling what he had in there to shut me up.

"Kyra! Hey!" He mocked my high pitch. "I didn't think you remembered me when you didn't speak at Applebee's. I know you saw me."

"I'm sorry. I was out with my family. You know how that can be." I tried to sound as apologetic as humanly possible, noticing I was stuck between Chris and the dumpster.

"No, I don't know how that can be. I don't have any kids. Can you guess why?" He was slowly closing the space between us with his tall, wiry frame. I was scared of what he might do, but happy at the same time thinking about the night I left him crying in his back seat. I wasn't saying anything so Chris took both hands and slammed them on the dumpster lid. He was two inches from my face breathing heavily. "You almost *bit-my-dick off*." I remembered the night vividly- as I'm sure he did. I did what I had to do to protect myself. Never would I have thought that night would come back to bite me in the ass. I didn't know what to say. The thought of apologizing profusely came to me, but no words escaped my lips. "You owe me some ass." He spit. I couldn't believe what was happening. He almost growled, "Now I gotta make you bleed." Those words gave me a painful flashback of cowering under the covers, hoping my father would stay out of my room. He had said that to me once- *now I gotta make you bleed.* And I didn't fight him, I gave in. But I wasn't that girl anymore and I'd be damned if I was letting Chris get what he wanted.

I looked him dead in his eyes determined to beat him again. He grabbed me by my arms trying to shake fear into me. When I still didn't cry or give in, he got even angrier.

"Oh so you think you bad? I know you still want me. You probably thought about me every day, didn't you?" Fear was working me over triple time, but I couldn't let him see me waver. He had me messed up.

"You're still stuck on something that happened sixteen years ago?" I was trying to piss him off even more, knowing if he would've left me barren I would've held on to that resentment until I died.

"Bitch *what*!" He threw me to the ground and my hand grazed something sharp. I acted like I was hurt and turned to see what it was. A broken beer bottle lay next to the dumpster.

"Get up and pull those pants down." I moved slowly to block his view of my hand grabbing the glass. "Bitch get up! I been waitin for this" He kicked me in my side and I winced from the blow, but I gripped the nose of the bottle with a sea of revenge roaring inside me.

"You ain't shit, Chris." I was rising slowly, planning my next move, taunting him.

"Who the hell do you think you talkin' to?" I was facing him now with the bottle behind my back.

"The same punk ass lil' boy who tried to rape me in the front seat of his car." He didn't say anything, just wrapped his fingers around my neck. I was taken back to a day I'd tried to block from my mind. A little girl who'd been abused too much had had enough. At that moment, I was her all over again. The urges that possessed her coursed through my veins, overpowering my morals. I could feel all her anger and fury flowing through me. She was inside me, taunting me. *Anybody that hurts us has got to go.* I was slipping into unconsciousness, but it was that little girl's wrath that propelled my arm, and the bottle, into the side of Chris's head. Dropping to his knees, he made a monstrous noise and grabbed his head. I was in shock and threw the glass to the ground. Watching him moan in pain wasn't as satisfying as I'd thought it would be. The groaning slowed and I still couldn't take my eyes off him.

He reached out to me with a bloody hand and I quickly scooted away. *"You- killed- me..."* he muttered. I snapped. Something in me went haywire and I kicked him in the face. I felt the mixture of soft flesh and hard bone through my Nike's as I stomped him over and over again until I realized he was no longer moving.

Shaking my father's image from my mind, I tried to work quickly to get cleaned up. I threw away my trash bags, took off my tennis shoes, picked up the glass and ran back into the house.

JaLea was still asleep as I undressed and stuffed everything in a plastic bag. After I showered, I sat naked on the den floor with the bag in my lap. What the hell would I do with it? The bottle had my prints and Chris's blood on it. My shoes were covered in blood and I couldn't wash them. I watched Law and Order enough to know I couldn't get rid of the blood. I never wanted to see those clothes again anyway. The only thing I could think of was throw each item out the window one at a time on the way to Atlanta.

Everything we were taking was already packed in the car. JaLea and I would be leaving from Denny's after breakfast so I figured we should go ahead and leave the house. I couldn't sit around waiting for Chris's body to be found and police wanting to question everyone in the neighborhood. When I got some clean clothes on, I shook JaLea awake and sent her out to the car. Then I closed and locked the front door to a house that held so many memories but was no longer mine.

153

***

"Hey Mama!" I almost made her jump out of her house shoes the next morning.

"What in God's name are you doing here?" she asked.

"I decided I wanted to spend my last night here in the house I grew up in," I lied. I hadn't slept a wink. I had murdered two men and they haunted me all night. I was scared to close my eyes because of my dreams, but I saw them everywhere anyway, pointing and poking at me. They threatened rape, threw insults, and cursed me for their deaths. If Mama could tell I hadn't slept all night, she kept it to herself.

When we got to Denny's at eight, it was already packed. Everyone was in high spirits and I tried my best. We didn't stay at breakfast long because JaLea and I had to be on our way. By 9:30, we were crying our goodbyes. I felt guilty thinking about Aaron while I was saying goodbye to Mama. It wasn't that I felt I needed to say goodbye to him. But he'd been a part of me since high school. He was the father of my only child, but he could never be a part of our lives.

Once on the road, I started thinking. There hadn't been many men that had crossed my path, but they had all fallen painfully from grace. I was forced to protect myself from my father by murdering him, Reggie had been murdered at seventeen, Aaron, the love of my life, was a crack fiend and Chris's body would probably be on a slab in the morgue in no time. I convinced myself that it wasn't me, that I just had bad luck and my luck would change in Atlanta. It would be a whole new start for me and my daughter.

I looked over at her sleeping peacefully. Smiling, I reached to the back, opened up the plastic bag, let down my window and threw out the first shoe.

THIRTY-ONE

"Mama, I love it here!" JaLea came running into the dining room with her cousin. "Camille took me to Lennox Square Mall and I wanted to pass out! St. Louis ain't got nothin' on Atlanta. The malls are better, people dress so different, I haven't seen a raggedy car yet and Mama, the *boys*!"

"Watch yourself." Camille laughed as I cut JaLea off. The last thing I wanted to hear was her going on about some nappy headed lil' boys. The two girls looked like sisters running back out the door. Both were tall and overdeveloped for sixteen with deep brown skin and hazel eyes.

"Girl, those two together... we gone have somethin' serious on our hands. Fine as they think they are." Annette sat across from me at the dining room table. "Need a break?" she asked. I looked down at the table and laughed. I hadn't wasted time contacting the clients Annette had lined up for me and I was already swamped with papers full of party ideas and color swatches. We'd only been in Atlanta two full days.

"Yeah, I could use a break." I pushed some papers off to the side and Annette handed me a Pepsi.

"So..." she paused. I knew what was coming by her hesitance. I'd been waiting for her to ask for more details as to why I uprooted my teenage daughter and moved all the way to Atlanta... without my husband. "What's up?" she asked. I laughed at her.

"You know you nosy, right?" I joked.

"I'm sorry, it's eatin' at me. You know nosiness runs in the family!" I laughed again even though it really wasn't a laughing matter. I briefly explained to her what Aaron had been through and the fact that he owed all that money.

"And they expected *you* to pay it?" she asked.

"Yeah, and I can't. Scratch that, I *won't*."

"Your husband needs his ass beat."

"Who you tellin'?" I got up to throw both our Pepsi cans away as she lit up a cigarette. "I'm so stressed I could almost smoke one of those things."

"You don't want one of these," she stated getting up. "I normally don't smoke in the house but I just got pissed off." I shook my head watching her step out onto the patio.

Her house was amazing. The front door opened into a foyer full of exotic looking plants and family portraits. The living room sat to the immediate left and was decorated with pure white furniture, sleek glass tables with gold accents, pale lavender walls and more plants and pictures. The downstairs bathroom was off to the right of the short hall and beyond that was the doorway to a common area stretching the full length of the house. On the east side was the family room with three comfortable, cushy couches facing a ridiculously huge television. On the west side was the kitchen. The oak cabinets, green marble countertops and stainless steel oven were spotless, almost as if no one ate there. But the lingering smell of chicken and seasoning gave it away. Behind the pantry doors were endless cans of Glory Greens, soups, vegetables, boxes of Jiffy cornbread mix, Rice-a-Roni, Zatarains and pastas, and the refrigerator was full to its capacity. Between the den and kitchen areas was the dining room with a round oak table, four high-backed chairs with melon colored cushions, and matching place mats. The patio where Annette stood was adjacent to the dining room.

The blinds stayed open letting in the Atlanta sun, and for

a few minutes I sat there soaking it all in. I amazed myself, the things I was able accomplish in the past week. I smiled remembering the last few moments with Mama and Tasha. Then I felt selfish. Did I really have to move *so* far away? By leaving, had I put them in the line of fire? Would they get harassed like JaLea and I had? Would that man do to Mama what he'd done to me?

"Snap out of it." Annette had put her cigarette out and was on her way back in. "I know you're in a messed up situation but you gotta snap outta that sweetheart. JaLea needs you to be stronger than that.*"*

I watched her head toward the stairs across from the bathroom, waiting until she disappeared to make my daily calls.

"Hey, baby!" Mama didn't even say hello when she answered.

"Hey, Mama." I was just checking on her. I'd already spent the past couple of days rambling on about my clients, how beautiful Atlanta was and how happy JaLea was. We'd all been to Annette's house before so there was no surprise there. I was all talked out.

"You know Tasha's had people over already looking at your stuff. I grabbed a couple of things for myself if you don't mind."

"I don't mind, Mama." My mind was elsewhere. Why hadn't either Tasha or Mama said anything to me about Chris? It was too far fetched to think that he was actually still lying in the alley after three days. Surely had he been found it would've made it to the news. My old neighborhood wasn't exactly the upscale Central West End, but it was nice enough to attract media attention if a black man had been found stabbed with a beer bottle and beaten to death.

I wasn't about to push the issue.

"Well I was just checking in, Mama. I gotta call Tasha and see how things are going."

"Okay, love you."

"Love you too." We hung up and Chris was still on my mind. I was thinking about coming up with a story to get Tasha out into the alley behind my house. She wouldn't tie him to me if she found him there. Surely she wouldn't remember him after all those years, if in fact he was still laying between the dumpsters. Reluctantly, I decided to leave well enough alone.

"Hello?" Tasha answered her cell phone sounding tired and thirsty.

"Hey heffa, stop workin' so hard," I joked, looking at the clock. It was almost one. Knowing Tasha, she'd probably been at the house or up and running all day.

"I haven't been to work today."

"What's wrong?" She sounded funny.

"Nothing."

"Don't lie to me Tasha." She hesitated.

"I'm in the hospital." Images flashed through my head at the speed of light.

A faceless man with a knife to Tasha's neck, a drive-by past her University City home...bullet holes disfiguring a face... a lifeless body in an alley... a young girl raped to the point of numbness... bright, red blood soiling plush white carpet...

"What happened?"

"Aaron happened," she said.

THIRTY-TWO

"Aaron?" I was confused. "What do you mean *Aaron* happened?" There was a pause on the line. "Tasha?"

"I didn't wanna tell you. You've got enough on your plate."

"Tasha, talk to me." I braced myself for whatever was coming.

"Okaaay," she whined like a five year old in trouble. "I went to the house to pick up Aaron's things and he caught me on the way back out. I guess he'd been watching from somewhere because he asked me why I'd been moving boxes and wanted to know where you were." I could sense where she was going. "You know I wasn't about to tell him you were gone, so I lied. I came up with something about the house getting painted and you and JaLea being at your mom's. He said I was lying and that your car hadn't been in front of your mom's. He was pissed, Kyra. I mean he looked *really* bad. He grabbed the box and threw it down and his clothes fell out. He said, 'Oh, ya'll tryin' to move me out?' Then he pushed me up against my car and I tried to get away but he grabbed my hair and slammed my head on the window. I tried to kick him or do something to hurt him but he pulled me back and said, 'Tell Kyra's ass that she belongs to me. Always has, always will.' He threw me down and I hit my head on the sidewalk and he just walked off like nothing happened."

"Oh my God, Tasha, I'm so sorry. I didn't mean for

anybody else to get hurt." It amazed me how extremely different Aaron was. I thought it was impossible to lose any more faith in him, but he had proved me wrong.

"Don't apologize for his ass, Kyra. What he's doing is *not* your fault!" she screamed angrily. "Aaron is through. Cut your losses." I apologized again, even though she didn't want me to, and we ended the conversation with her words heavy on my mind. *Aaron is through.* I knew she was right, I knew I needed to move on.

"Annette!" I called up the stairs. She looked down at me from the second floor balcony.

"What?"

"Let's go to Lennox." I needed to get my mind off Aaron. There were other fish in the sea. Sexy fish with smooth skin and deep pockets who spoke with a southern drawl.

"*You* wanna go to Lennox?"

"Why did you say it like that? '*You* wanna go to Lennox?'"

"Lennox is upscale. *You* are still stuck in St. Louis sweetie."

"Well give me something to wear! Besides, if Lennox is all you and JaLea make it out to be, then I know I can find a decent man there." I sashayed in circles through the hall until Annette made it downstairs. "A man huh?" she teased. "Let's go then."

We never made it to the mall.

After I was done raking my hair, I went back to the dining room and I noticed I had three missed calls from Tasha. Before I could call back, the phone was ringing again.

"Kyra!" she yelled once I answered.

"Tasha what's wrong?"

"A man came to my room saying Aaron owed him money and you were supposed to pay him back. I don't know if he was watching you or Aaron told him you were gone, but he knows and he's highly pissed." She was scared as hell; I could hear it in her voice. "He said if you don't show up on your front porch with his money by noon tomorrow he's gonna start hurting folks."

The room went pitch black. I should've known moving to Atlanta would only help JaLea and I. I didn't take the time to think about the people I left in St. Louis.

"Okay... uhh..." my mind was spinning. I had the money but I'd promised Mama I wouldn't pay Aaron's debt with what she gave me. *Damn that!* I needed to take care of business and if Mama got mad at me then so be it. She'd get over it. "When are you getting out?' I asked Tasha.

"I'm just here for observation. I should be home in a couple hours. I been here all morning."

"Well, if I come can I stay with you tonight? I don't even want Mama to know I'm in St. Louis. She'll suspect something."

"That's not even a question. You know you can stay with me."

"Mama," JaLea scared the hell out of me. I jumped like I was caught with my hand in the cookie jar. "You're going back to St. Louis? For what?"

"None of your business and what did I tell you about eavesdropping?"

"Sorry Mama. Can I go?"

"No!" She jumped back, startled. I hadn't meant to yell at her. I had gotten stressed out just that quick. And I was scared, terrified that no matter what I did I could never get away from my past and the decisions I'd made. No matter how much I paid Aaron's drug dealer, he had connected the two of us and always would. I could tell him I didn't care, try my best to convince him that Aaron and I weren't together. Then my family would become fair game.

"Is somethin' wrong, Mama?"

"Nothin' sweetie." I tried to calm myself down so she would forget the whole situation. She stared at me, her eyes searching for the truth. I knew she didn't believe me, but she was the daughter and I was her Mama and I didn't owe her an explanation. "I'll be back late tomorrow," was all I said before hurrying past her.

After I'd packed a couple of changes of clothes, I looked for JaLea to say goodbye but she was nowhere to be found. I figured she was upset and hiding from me, so I stopped in to tell Annette I had some business to take care of.

"Damn! I just found you an outfit. How did we get from going to the mall to you going all the way back to St. Louis?"

"There are just some loose ends I gotta tie up. JaLea's okay, right?"

"Girl go 'head. JaLea's fine."

JaLea was not fine. She was stubborn just like her father. When it was time for me to leave she still hadn't come out of her hiding place, so I gave up. I cursed myself all the way up Highway 75 for being just as stubborn and not looking for her more. But I needed to get to St. Louis. I didn't have time to cater to her teenage hormones. They could wait until I got to Tasha's house.

The ride went quicker than I'd expected. Running on fear and adrenaline alone, I didn't get sleepy or lonely. I wanted to get the transaction over with and move on. The thought crossed my mind that as long as Aaron was alive, and doing the things he was doing, the people I cared about would never be safe. I shook the thought from my mind as I pulled into Tasha's driveway.

Before I could get to the door, I heard a creak come from behind my truck. The hatch was lifting slowly and I froze. I wanted to run and bang on the front door but, at the same time, I needed to see what was going on.

When JaLea jumped out from behind the truck, I almost

took my belt off and beat her sixteen-year-old ass.

"Heffa if I had a gun you would've been shot!" She just stood there in her tank, shorts and flip flops looking like a deer caught in the headlights. I went and snatched her by her arm. "You must be crazy." I told her dragging her to the door. "Only somebody crazy would hide in the back of a damn SUV for eight hours!"

"I had a bad feeling about you coming here alone," she whined as I knocked.

"You what!" I yelled just as Tasha swung the door open.

"What is the problem?" she asked. I hadn't realized that I'd been banging on the door.

"Apparently, I got a stowaway." I told her.

"We- well hurry up and come in," she stammered, obviously not expecting JaLea to be with me. Once we were behind the closed doors she said, "A car's been circling the block for the past half hour. It's making me nervous." She peeked out the front window and I turned to avoid JaLea's I-told-you-so stare.

"Man, I left something in the car." I shook my head at my own forgetfulness. The two thousand dollars was stuffed in a brown envelope and tucked in the glove compartment. That kind of money needed to be watched at all times.

"Be careful, Mama." JaLea and Tasha stood watch at the front door. The night fell quiet as I listened to my inner thoughts.

I had a bad feeling... a car's been circling the block... be careful Mama...

My hands fumbled with my keys as I jogged to the car. I was trippin' bad. I'd been to Tasha's house hundreds of times so I couldn't figure out what the problem was. Maybe JaLea's 'bad feeling' had rubbed off on me. As soon as I got the key into the lock, Tasha and JaLea were screaming for me.

"Mama!"

"Kyra!" I spun away from the car so fast my eyes barely

had time to focus on the man that had ran up the driveway from the street.

"Remember me, bitch?"

"*NO*! Mama *RUN*!" I could see Tasha struggling to pull JaLea into the house. The image was as clear and unnerving as the .45 being pointed at me.

I didn't have a chance to think before the hot steel exploded into my chest. I flew back into the truck and slid down to the cool concrete.

"Bet you never expected to see *me* again. Left me in a gotdamn alley to die! You must've lost yo fuckin' mind. You learned a good lesson now didn't you?"

My chest was a volcano with hot lava spilling out. I may have lost control of my bowels but, at that point, it didn't even matter. The ear blasting screams coming from Tasha and JaLea were dwindling into the background and Chris's smiling face became a dot in my fading vision. The pain was subsiding and an eerie peace was taking over. I'd felt my life slipping away before. It was painful and unbearable. But the feeling I had at that moment… it was intense and inviting, almost addictive. I'd spent most of my life trying to outrun my demons, knowing full well that one day they would catch up to me. That time, though, there was nothing to pull me back.

PART FOUR

breakthrough

THIRTY-THREE

I held my mama while she bled to death from a gunshot wound to the chest. I prayed while my crack head father acted a hot mess at the funeral, screaming and trying to climb in the damn casket. They say you can always weed out the guilty.

I guess my parents thought I was too young or just too immature to understand the fact that my mama went broke because of my father's addiction. I overheard mama talking about my father cheating… with another crack head no less! And just in case that wasn't bad enough, he brought the hoe to the funeral! Even though I'd never personally seen anyone strung out, it was painfully obvious that those two were far beyond that checkpoint. I had to try my hardest to act like I didn't see him acting a gotdamn fool. As far as I was concerned, he was the reason my mama was gone in the first place. He didn't have *shit* to say to me.

My aunt Tasha practically had to beg me to go to the funeral. I would've been fine staying at home, not having to watch people I didn't know showing their asses. Tasha said I needed a chance to say goodbye. I told her I'd already said my goodbyes that August night covered in my mama's blood.

After mama died, my grandma lost her mind… literally. When Tasha broke the news to her, I stood back studying grandma's face. It was expressionless, the calm before the storm. She refused help as she busied herself with funeral arrangements, informing family members, and planning the repast.

My head was still pounding from crying my eyes out when I headed to the kitchen to check on grandma. She was still posted up pretending to cook, even though we had more than enough. The table was lined with chicken, greens, macaroni and cheese, candied yams and dressing. Chocolate cake, apple crisp and two sweet potato pies sat on the kitchen table and everybody was reminiscing on happier times. Grandma was leaning against the stove with her fingers at her temples. I couldn't help but wish I could've put my pain aside because I knew as well as she seemed to be holding it together, inside she was ten times worse.

Then the inevitable happened, the breakdown we'd all feared. Grandma picked up the pot of greens and threw it against the wall. She took one look at the mess on the floor and started screaming. Not crying, just high pitched, scary movie, ear piercing screaming. It went on for forty-five agonizing minutes. She'd stop for a moment, leading everyone to think she was about to calm down, then she'd start up again.

During the next couple of weeks, Tasha basically moved in. Grandma wouldn't leave her room or even speak, and it took both of us to get her in the tub. Between Tasha working and me starting school, there was no one there during the day and we'd come home to an unbearable smell. It came to a point where neither of us could take it. We ended up having her committed and I moved my stuff in with Tasha.

It's been over two years and grandma hasn't uttered a word.

Tasha became my paranoid warden. Every move I made, everything I did, everyone I *tried* to hang out with, was subject to her scrutiny. Living with her was boot camp! Wake, wash, eat, school, home, homework, eat, sleep- everyday. I had no freedom whatsoever. The warden thought whoever killed my mother would come after me. I told her if that was the case, he'd be after her too since we both saw that demon's face. Besides, if he was trippin' off leaving witnesses, he would've taken care of us that night too. Instead, we were left to live in this hell on Earth.

I thought out my suicide more than once. Jumping off an overpass, running in front of a bus, ramming Tasha's car into the side of a building... anything. I just wanted to ease the pain. Since Tasha never let me out, I had way too much time to think about why I wanted to end my life. My father was somewhere strung out, my mother had been murdered right in front of my face, and my grandma had gone crazy. The handful of people who I thought were my friends turned out to be nosy and fake. I was never given the opportunity to meet people outside of school because of Tasha's insecurities. She was the only somebody I had left and she chose to piss me off.

It took a while to pull it together, but I got tired of moping around and feeling sorry for myself. I had to tell myself, as harsh as it sounded, that people died all the time and it's not always expected. The only thing I would've accomplished by taking my life would've been to further hurt the people who were already upset by my mother's murder. I felt selfish as hell and I knew I had to live my life and make my mama proud.

I made a vow to myself that, if I didn't do anything else, I'd make sure the bastard who killed my mother would pay for what he did. It would take some doing, but it was something that needed to be done. I didn't care how long it took or how many people I had to piss off. That man's eyes were burned into my memory for an eternity. I felt in my heart that one day I would find him and have him punished. That would be a thousand pounds of burden lifted off my shoulders and my mama could rest in peace.

Until I could hash out a plan, I needed to do something, anything to keep myself sane. Once I graduated high school, I began to reinvent myself. I vowed that the money my mama left me would be strictly for college so, despite Tasha's protests, I got a full time job at Body Central. I spent almost half of each check filling my closet with the outfits from their magazines. I chopped my hair off in sexy spikes, practiced walking in heels, and studied Tasha when she arched her eyebrows. I spent the whole summer perfecting a personality that wasn't my own. The old JaLea was a shy turtle hiding in her shell, still mourning over the death of her mother. She didn't care about hair, clothes, or even her own life.

By the time I made it to Tureman College, I'd evolved into an outspoken flirt who was sexy as hell. My reassurance came during freshman orientation. Watching guys drool over me, not even attempting to hide their horny stares from their girlfriends, was a rush. It had been so long since I'd gotten that kind of attention that I almost forgot how good it felt. I commanded that damn room! Sure I'd spent almost twenty minutes in the bathroom trying to keep myself from having a panic attack, but it paid off. All eyes were on me and I was lovin' that shit!

I scanned the cafeteria trying to see if anybody sexy caught my eye. There were a lot of cute dudes but one was fine as that *thang*! His skin was caramel and he had soft curls on top of his head. He was sitting at the table alone so I strolled over to him like my heart wasn't beating a thousand times a minute. He looked up at me with the sexiest hazel eyes I'd ever seen and my panties got wet. I imagined his dick getting hard under the table and him throwing me on top of it and taking my virginity right there in the middle of the presentations. He invited me to have a seat instead. I was so nervous and wet I could've sworn my juices were running down my legs, but I sat down anyway.

"Hey… Terrell." I repeated the name I saw on the tacky name tag they'd insisted everyone wear.

"Hey…" he hesitated.

"Juh-lee-ya." I cut him off before he butchered my

name.

"JaLea," he repeated. "That's sexy." He grinned and a dimple dug into his right cheek. *Too fine*!

"So what are we even doing here? I'm sure we can get to know each other just fine without having to listen to them talk all day." I nodded toward the speaker at the front. I didn't know where the words were coming from and I wondered if he assumed I was asking him to leave the cafeteria wit me. After all, I knew what freshman orientation was for anyway.

"They just wanna make sure we know the ropes I guess." He laughed nervously and I realized he was trippin' just as much as I was. That put me at ease a little.

"So why are you here, in hick ass Clamon, IL?" I asked him.

"They showed me the money. And anything was better than stayin' home."

"And where's home?"

"St. Louis." My jaw dropped.

"Me too!" I almost yelled. There was that dimple again. The conversation was smooth sailing from there. I flirted with him like my life depended on it, trying my best to bring attention to my chest, even though my tube top was doing that all on its own. I even went and sat beside him so close our thighs were touching. *I had him*! I was scared out of my mind and didn't know what the hell to *do* with him… but nonetheless, I had him.

Terrell and I became good friends, studying together almost every night, eating together, even going out to the lil' rinky-dink club, Booker's. So many females were jealous because Terrell's fine ass paid them no attention when he was with me. When he got all dressed up and smelling good…*mmm, mmm, mmm*… There were so many times I wanted to tell him to just take his clothes off so we could do the damn thang! I always held my tongue though. After sweating up against him all night at Booker's, I'd go back to my room, alone. My sophomore roommate thought she was too good to room with a freshman so she stayed with her boyfriend. I didn't give a damn. I took my mama's decorating genes and turned my double into a single… where I masturbated every night.

Shame what such a short period of time had done to me. When I got to Tureman, I was posing, pretending to be something I wasn't. A couple of months later and I'm a walking hormone, flirting with every guy that crossed my path no matter what. I just liked to see that stupid, horny look on their faces. I made sure the clothes I wore made everybody say DAMN! And if they said it in a negative way then they were hatin' because I always look good. I thought about sex like a man, even contemplated buying a porno or two. I decided against it though. Clamon was too small to go around buying pornos all willie-nillie. I could feel the heartbeat between my legs whenever I watched the guys get crunk at Booker's. But Terrell… he set me on fire! I wanted to lick all six feet, two inches of him! I wanted to ride him until my legs went limp. I wanted to *make love* to him and it scared the hell outta me.

THIRTY-FOUR

JaLea's long legs stretched up to thick thighs that disappeared underneath her denim mini. Gladiator sandals showed off her pedicured toes and her 34 D's sat up and alert in the tight, orange tank top. She twirled the tip of her belt in her French tipped fingers and had the other hand on a curvy hip. Her waist was the only thing on her that was small. She stood at a statuesque 5'8" without heels and topped her height off with a short Halle Berry do. Accentuated with liner and fake lashes, her hazel eyes popped. The fullness of her lips was enhanced with lip gloss but barely outshined her perfect deep mocha skin.

Two months before, she was the sexy new girl. Now, to the guys, she was "The Tease", to the haters, she was "The Bitch", and to the gay boys, she was "Queen Diva", but to Terrell, she was just JaLea. Beautiful, flashy JaLea who'd demanded his attention and stolen his heart. Flirtatious JaLea who had Terrell dreaming about her from the first day of freshman orientation. Intelligent JaLea who kept his mind clicking on way more than history during their study sessions.

Terrell would try desperately to focus in class, but his mind always wandered back to JaLea. He was afraid he was beginning to incur a sort of sick infatuation with her. Every aspect of her being kept him fantasizing about her becoming his personal, chocolate playboy bunny; her tall thickness, the way her clothes hugged her curves, her eccentric personality, the way she did something new and crazy to her hair all the time, the way she radiated energy with every step she took... he even adored the emphasis on her r's that was much like his own St. Louis drawl. He was addicted to JaLea's femininity. She carried herself like her pussy was made of platinum, like it did magic tricks, hypnotizing any man fortunate enough to get a taste of her sweet juice. He was that lucky man in his seductive imagination:

JaLea answered the door in nothing but a pair of stilettos. The red strings wrapped up her ebony calves and tied underneath her knees. She backed up, did a 360°, and awaited his approval. The sudden bulge in his pants was compliment enough. He smiled, giddy as a kid in a candy store, taking in the beauty of her round breasts, her nipples, erect, waiting to be pinched between his teeth. Her perfectly trimmed forest made his mouth water and he wanted desperately to bury his face between her healthy thighs. Instead he watched as she turned away from him, strolled to the bed and climbed onto the pure white, satin sheets, sticking her apple bottom teasingly in the air. He tore his clothes off, unable to stand her prancing around any longer. He eased onto the bed behind her and didn't waste time giving her long, hard strokes that she felt in her stomach. When he stopped to take a breath, he pulled her over on top of him and let his eyes roll back as she rocked her hips the way she did when she walked. Within moments, her body was convulsing and he exploded inside her. Screams of pleasure resonated through the small room and they both rolled over, exhausted from their sexual escapade.

Terrell's imagination got the best of him sometimes. He'd build himself up so much that when he snapped back into reality he'd have to take a trip to the bathroom to relieve himself. The truth flattened him like a cartoon anvil. JaLea was his friend, nothing more. Sure, she flirted with him all the time, but that was her m.o. Flirting, to her, was reflex, a profession that she had mastered. A smile from her would have any guy on the campus hard for the rest of the day. But Terrell didn't care how many minds she toyed with. He wanted to change all that, to finally make his dreams about JaLea come true. He wanted her all to himself and didn't care how many hoops he had to jump through to get to her. She'd haunted his dreams for two months and he was tired of it. He was tired of watching her flounce around campus knowing she didn't belong to him. He was tired of all the late night study sessions leading only to him closing himself in the bathroom to work out his wrists and keep from getting blue balls.

He couldn't help thinking JaLea knew what she was doing. She had to know she was driving him crazy. His poker face was nonexistent. He couldn't hide his attraction to her or his longing to be with her every waking moment. There was no mistake that she was the most sought after freshman on campus, but, as far as Terrell was concerned, JaLea belonged to him. Everything from her spiked hair and luscious lips to her suckable toes and ridiculously sexy body.

Terrell felt like he needed JaLea, like she'd awakened something in him he never knew existed. It was scary and exciting and he knew he couldn't settle for just being her friend anymore. He wanted to hold her on his lap and paint her neck with kisses. He wanted to spoil her because in his eyes she deserved any and everything she wanted. He wanted to run into her in the cafeteria and be able to slip his arms around her waist and bend over to kiss her ear. No one else would matter once he made JaLea his woman; and he would stop at nothing to make sure he felt the same way. He wouldn't stop until he knew everything there was to know about JaLea Washington.

THIRTY-FIVE

Terrell was lookin' sexy as usual when I ran into him at breakfast. He grinned, showing his pearly whites, and pulled out a chair for me.

"Mornin' beautiful," he said. I sat down with my omelet trying to shake sex from my mind.

"Hey, sexy," I replied back. "What'chu got planned for Thanksgiving break?"

"My people always cook for Thanksgiving. How about you?" I hesitated. It wasn't until then that I realized in the couple of months Terrell and I had been kickin' it, we hadn't really discussed our families. I knew he grew up with his great grandparents, he knew I stayed with my aunt. Bottom line. He knew nothing about my mother's murder, my crack head father, my crazy grandmother, or my 'summer transformation'. I should've been able to tell him, especially with all the feelings I had for him.

"JaLea? You goin' home for Thanksgiving?" I was stuck! *Say something damnit!*

"Uh, yeah, I'm going home. But my aunt and I don't really celebrate Thanksgiving. We hardly even eat together at all." Holidays had lost all meaning. I laughed nervously but Terrell didn't think it was funny.

"You wanna come to my house? You gotta have a real meal on Thanksgiving. And my grandma can throw down on some candy yams!"

"Okay," I answered before thinking twice. It would've been different if I wasn't head over heels in love with him. If I'd just wanted to have sex with him, I could easily go to his house and eat instead of being cooped up in the house with Tasha and nothing to do. But that wasn't the case. I was putting on a front, trying to act like I didn't want him when I did. Probably more than he wanted me. I was just too damn scared to take that next step. Taking the next step meant opening up to Terrell, letting him in on all my painful secrets. I wasn't scared to say it out loud, I was terrified of what his reaction might be.

"That's cool. You can ride back to St. Louis with me... if that's okay with you."

"Can you handle being alone with me?" I bit my bottom lip and cocked my head sideways.

"We study together almost every night and I manage." He grinned at me.

"Yeah, but we have books to keep us company. Once we get in that car, it'll just be us." My heart sped up its pace and I zoomed in between his legs with my dick-vision. He was hard.

"I like the sound of that... just us." He went there again and it made the hairs on my neck stand at attention. Terrell and I were in our own little world until it was time to go to class. He rambled on about how I was going to love his grandma's cooking. I listened intently, happy to hear him talk, but antsy about the trip to come.

***

Even though Thanksgiving break was a week away, I started packing right after my last class. A knock at the door broke me from my trance. "Who is it?" I asked, sorting through my closet.

"Terrell." *Damn!* I didn't want him to see me stressed about *packing*.

"Just a minute!" I stuffed everything I had out into my suitcase and shoved it under the bed. When I opened the door,

Terrell held out a single rose. "For me?" I squealed.

"Who else, beautiful?" I loved the way he called me 'beautiful' like it was my name. I took the flower and put it to my nose, moving over so Terrell could step in. "Look, we gotta talk." Uh-oh. He looked serious so I wiped the stupid grin off my face and sat on the bed. He sat across from me at the desk.

"What's wrong?"

"This... us." I squinted at him and frowned. What the hell did that mean? *This... us.* He must've seen the look on my face because he cleared his throat with a quickness and kept going. "JaLea, you gotta know how I feel about you. And no matter how bad you try to play hard to get, you feel the same way." He was staring at me and I couldn't look away. I should've expected that the conversation would come sooner or later. I'd been hoping for later. "I'm tired of beatin' around the bush. I don't know why I waited so long in the first place. I been thinkin' about this all day. Thinkin' about *you* all day. *I invited you to my house to meet my family for Thanksgiving*! I have *never* invited a female to my house. You are *that* important to me."

"After two months, Terrell?" It was the first thing I could think to say, and it was dumb as hell. There he was pouring his heart out and, knowing I felt the same way, the only thing I could think to do was doubt him.

"Stop lyin' to me. And to yourself." He got up and pulled me off the bed to him. "Look me in the eyes and tell me you don't wanna be wit me." I couldn't do it. He had me with those beautiful hazel things. Then it happened. He lifted my chin, bent down and kissed me. I'd kissed a few boys before and felt a little somethin', but Terrell was settin' off bombs! I was caught up, and when I felt his arms slip around my waist, I almost fainted. My knees felt a little weak, but I wrapped my arms around his neck to hold myself up. His kiss was everything I'd imagined since I had first laid eyes on him. I was wondering what the sex would be like, what it would be like to lose my virginity to him. When his hands slid down over my butt, I immediately cut the kiss short and backed away.

"JaLea..." I couldn't look at him. He put his hand under my chin to tilt my face towards his. "Okay. We can take it slow. I just want you to be mine," he repeated. Hugging him was all the answer he needed and he squeezed me tighter.

***

My secrets were eating at me for the rest of the week. By the time Terrell knocked on my door to pick me up, I'd made up my mind to tell him everything. I took advantage of the twelve mile road that led out of Clamon. By the time we got on Highway 55, Terrell knew everything from the day Shandi Bradshaw almost overdosed at my sixteenth birthday party to the day I sat at this table during freshman orientation.

"I'm really sorry about your mom," he started. "But why were you scared to tell me? You didn't do nothin' wrong. Nothin' that happened was your fault." He took one hand off the wheel and put it on my thigh.

"I need your help." The words came out before I could stop myself.

"Help with what?" He put his hand back on the wheel and kept his eyes on the road.

"I need to know who killed my mama."

"I thought you said it was your father's dealer."

"I *think* so. But whether it was or not, he still hasn't paid for what he did. If I ever see him again I swear..."

"JaLea..." he cut me off. "I understand you want this guy caught but don't you think it's dangerous for *you* to try and catch him?"

"I saw his face, Terrell. He looked right at me. I'm tired of thinking I see him everywhere! Every time I try to think about my mama, all I see is her getting killed. I can't rest til' I do somethin' about it!" We sat in silence for the next few minutes.

"If it's that important to you, I'll help you." He didn't have as attitude and wasn't sarcastic at all. He was genuinely willing to help and I was eager to take advantage. "I hated living with my great grandparents," he blurted out. I looked over at him but his eyes stayed focused ahead. "It felt like I was never there. I was invisible. They were too old to try and raise me anyway." His jaws clenched as the anger of his past seeped into the present. My curiosity got the better of me and, since we were sharing, I decided to dig deeper.

"What happened to your parents?" He wasn't alarmed. It seemed as though he'd been expecting that question all along.

"My mama is a basket case. I've only seen her a couple times 'cause she was locked up most of my life. I saw my dad once, or at least I'm pretty sure it was him. Last year I was walking to the corner store. I saw my mama yellin' at some dude but his back was turned and I couldn't see his face. When she saw me she stopped talking and the dude turned to see what she was looking at." He took a deep breath and tightened his grip on the wheel before continuing. "It was like looking in a mirror, JaLea. Both of 'em just stared at me. I know my mama knew who I was, and that nigga had to. I look just like his ass!"

I wanted to hold him and tell him that he had me and I would never treat him like crap. I couldn't bring myself to be so mushy so I kept my mouth shut. When I looked over at him, he had a silly little grin on his face.

"What?" I asked, unable to keep myself from smiling too.

"As messed up as our lives were, we deserve each other!" I laughed, even though it really wasn't a laughing matter.

"Well, I never even knew my great grandparents. Yours must be in pretty good shape."

"Yeah, they're almost eighty now. They're hangin' in there. That's were Thanksgiving dinner is. My grandfather's been there since I was about ten, but all his attention was on them, not me."

"My mama never talked about her father."

"Never?"

"Nope. I asked my grandma about him once, but she acted like I didn't say anything so I left it alone."

"That's strange."

"So do you think your family will like me?" I decided to change the subject.

"Oh yeah. You'll get along real good with all my cousins and stuff." I was actually referring to his grandparents and great grandparents, but I decided to leave well enough alone. A nosier side of me wanted to know what was up with his parents. Why had his mother been locked up and why had he never met his father? I felt sick for secretly hoping his mother would show up at Thanksgiving dinner so I could see what kind of woman would abandon her own son.

THIRTY-SIX

I stood outside the house fumbling with my keys. Tasha's car was there and I did NOT feel like dealing with her. I was so caught up in kissing Terrell goodbye that I hadn't even paid attention until he pulled off. If I'd noticed her car was there, I would've made an excuse to stay with Terrell longer. Tasha had called to check on me so many times it almost felt like I'd never left St. Louis. She was the last person I wanted to see, but I had no other choice. Just as I built up enough nerve to unlock the door, it swung open and Tasha and I were face to face.

"JaLea!" she yelled and threw her arms around me. I almost pulled away but decided against it.

"Hi Tasha." She loosened her grip and held me at arms length.

"Look at you!" Kyra would be so proud!" Why did she have to bring up my mama? "How did you get home? I would've picked you up if you would've told me when you wanted to come."

"I got a ride with a friend." I intended to tell her as little as possible about Terrell.

"Oh. Is this *friend* a boy?"

"Yes." We stood in awkward silence for a moment. Tasha had never attempted to talk to me about boys or sex before and I prayed she wouldn't start.

"Well, I hope he's a nice boy." *What*? No interrogation? She threw me for a loop with that one. Maybe she'd practiced chillin' out a little since I'd been gone. "I gotta get to the grocery store." She rushed past me and I was happy to see her go.

The house was just the same as when I left it. I used to love spending time a Tasha's house, but, since my mama died, it disgusted me. The living room was *brown*. All different shades of brown. The carpet, the couches and pillows and the lamp shades. The tables, entertainment center and even the picture frames were wooden. I scrunched my nose up at a 5x7 of my parents and I. *Ancient history*. I wondered why the hell Tasha still had that picture up. And the driveway. I could've went the rest of my life without ever having to see that constant reminder again.

Once up the steps, I threw my suitcase down and plopped on the bed. It was stuffy but I really didn't feel like struggling with the window. Instead I closed my eyes and let my thoughts wander to Terrell. His lips felt so good on mine and his hands drove me crazy. Every time we kissed his hands explored me. I hadn't even realized my hands were in my pants until the shriek of the phone broke my trance.

"Hello?" I tried to sound sleepy hoping whoever it was would get the point and I could get back to what I was doing.

"Hey babe. I made it in." I grinned when I heard Terrell's voice.

"And you started missin' me in the ten minutes it took to get you home?"

"I started missin' you when I pulled off."

"Aww, ain't that *sweet*." I teased.

"I was wondering if I could take you out tonight. It could be our first date."

"We been out before, Terrell."

"Booker's does *not* count as going out. And Wal-Mart don't either!" We both laughed, thinking about the hole-in-the-wall club and the one store every small town is guaranteed to have.

"Where are we going?" I was giddy. The thought of going out alone with Terrell had me lying back on the pillow with my free hand pinching my nipples.

"I was thinking about going to Red Lobster and to that new comedy club on Washington. Then if you're not tired, maybe we can sit in Tower Grove Park and chill for a lil' bit."

"Sounds good." Terrell heard a calm and collected JaLea. The reality was, I had gotten so carried away with myself that my nipples were sore.

"I can pick you up at seven. That means you got a good five hours to get all sexy for me."

"I thought you knew all this was natural!" He laughed and all of a sudden I couldn't wait to see him. "Umm, my aunt isn't here if you wanna swing by now."

"Oh… you… um…" he stammered. He knew what I was implying and I dared him to turn me down. I'd waited eighteen years and I was too horny and wanted Terrell too damn bad. "I'm on my way. Give me twenty minutes."

When we hung up, I hurried out of my clothes and jumped in the shower. I tried not to get too excited, making sure my every nook and cranny was smothered in Sweet Temptation body wash. After I dried off, I slapped baby oil all over myself and dug my favorite bra and panty set out of my suitcase. Once I got it on, I debated answering the door just like that, in my hot pink lace thong and black and pink lace bra. *Too much.* I pulled on the tightest pair of jeans I could find and a short-sleeved, black, v-neck that was cut dangerously low. I was raking my curls when I heard his car pull up. One peek through the blinds set my hormones into overdrive.

Terrell had pulled up in his jet black Aveo and was on his way up the steps. I grinned to myself, noticing he'd changed clothes too. The doorbell startled me, almost as if I hadn't been expecting it. I damn near broke my neck trying to get down the steps, but I put on a confident face before I swung the door open.

Terrell's smile sent shock waves through me and I moved over to let him in. He seemed just as nervous as I was, even though it wouldn't have been his first time.

"You look nice," I managed to say.

"You too," he said.

"Thank you." I took a deep breath and jumped in. "You wanna come upstairs with me?" He scanned my body from head to toe and his thick lips parted in suspense, trying to find words worthy enough to accept my invitation. All I could think was soon those lips would be all over me.

His silent nervousness excited me and I headed up the steps, slowly taking my shirt off as I went. I turned in the middle of the staircase to slip off my bra and his mouth hung wide open. He came towards me and I backed up playfully. Leading him to my bedroom where we kissed and undressed each other. His body was *amazing*! Smooth peanut butter skin, broad shoulders, washboard stomach and thick legs. I couldn't keep my eyes off the package he pulled out of his pants. I didn't know they could get that big!

"You okay?" Terrell broke my trance.

"Yeah, I'm good." I lied, second-guessing myself. My knees were buckling standing there staring at him. He was *gorgeous*, smart, funny as hell, and treated me like I held his world in the palm of my hands. I'd known him only three months and had decided to lose my virginity to him! What the hell was I thinking!

I didn't have a chance to pull back because his mouth was over mine, kissing me with so much passion that I couldn't help but react. My arms went around his neck and I pressed my body against him. He picked me up and took me over to the bed, breaking the kiss only after he had me lying down. We stared at each other for what seemed like forever.

"Terrell I- I've never done this before." I waited for his facial expression to change but his gaze never wavered.

"I'll be gentle with you." And he was. There wasn't an inch of my body his tongue didn't explore. By the time he wrapped my legs around his waist, I was shivering and more than ready. I couldn't catch my breath while he struggled his way inside me, and the first few strokes had me grabbing onto the back of Terrell's neck in pain. It took it all, even though I wanted to scream bloody murder. Our bodies rocked in unison for what felt like an eternity until pleasure shot through me. I had never felt anything like it. Terrell didn't stop his strokes. He lowered himself, kissing me until his body erupted in short, hard jerks. He rolled over and settled on his side, starring at me.

"What?" I asked, breathlessly.

"You- are incredible," he panted.

"*Incredible*, huh?" I smiled. I was trippin' off the fact that I'd lost my virginity to the sexy specimen next to me, and still had tingling between my legs where he'd been.

"You know you are," he answered. "Everything about you is perfect. I know this sounds crazy because we just met a few months ago, but you got in my head. The first day I met you, you had me. I never met anybody like you." My body tingled. I wanted to think of something, anything to say to him in return. The feelings I had wouldn't come out in words so I eased forward and wrapped my arms around him.

THIRTY-SEVEN

"I don't know if I like this," I told Terrell.

"Well I can't think of any other way to start," he answered, rubbing my thigh. It had taken him two days to talk me into going through my mama's things. So there we were sitting Indian-style on blankets in the basement. Everything she had was either donated or packed away in the twelve huge boxes we had sitting in front of us.

"You think we can get through it all before it's time to go back to school?" I asked him.

"If not, we can take the rest with us." I smiled at his reassurance and we each grabbed a box. I couldn't keep my eyes from wandering over to see what Terrell was looking at. I didn't wanna miss anything important.

"Babe…" He looked over at me. "This will go a lot quicker if we check our *own* boxes." I laughed and went back to the box in front of me.

"I just wanna make sure you're not overlooking anything important."

"Well if you want, you can recheck my boxes when we finish."

After two hours of purses, medical records, paycheck stubs, clothes, calendars, and other pointless crap, Terrell and I were exhausted.

"At least we're more than half way through." Terrell rubbed my shoulders once we made it up to the kitchen. I thought about the five unexplored boxes. We'd covered a lot of ground, but I groaned anyway. I washed my hands to make us a couple of sandwiches, and when I heard the front door, I groaned again. I wasn't deliberately trying to hide Terrell from Tasha, I was just hoping that I could. I didn't turn toward the kitchen door, I just kept making the sandwiches. The longer I waited, the faster my heart beat.

"JaLea, we really need to clean this house!" she yelled. I stayed still. "I just got some new cleaner and I-" She stopped at the entrance to the kitchen. I could hear her heels as they tapped across the linoleum and when she stopped beside me at the counter, I acted like she wasn't there. I poured koolaid for Terrell and I sat the sandwiches at the table. Finally, Tasha spoke.

"So who is this young man?"

"This is Terrell. I met him at Tureman…"

"Why are you two so dusty?" Tasha cut me off.

"How are you ma'am?" Terrell's good manners shined through Tasha's rudeness. I giggled in between bites and she glared at him before turning back to me.

"Why do you look like you've been playing in the basement?" she demanded.

"We have," I joked.

"Excuse me?" The sternness in her voice increased and I came to my senses.

"Terrell was helping me go through a few of mama's things."

"You had him all in my basement going through stuff in my house." *No she didn't!*

"The stuff in those boxes does *NOT* belong to you, though! They're more mine than anybody else's and if I wanna go through 'em with Terrell then that's exactly what I'll do." I grabbed Terrell's hand and pulled him towards the basement, leaving our half-eaten sandwiches on the table.

"What are you doin'?" Terrell asked, watching me move

the boxes at top speed.

"You heard how she snapped at me. I'm thinking there's something down here she doesn't want me to see."

"Okay, so why are we putting them back?" he asked grabbing a box.

"Not that one!" I yelled. "Put the ones back we looked through already. I'm gonna find a box to put all the things we think are important and we need to move this stuff before Tasha gets to it." We moved quickly, using the basement door to get to Terrell's car without having to pass Tasha.

It was quiet so I figured Terrell sensed how pissed I was. "How the hell could Tasha try to check *me* for going through *my* mama's stuff!? It's not like she's really any relation to us. She was just a friend who was lucky enough to get close to my family." Terrell kept quiet, letting me vent. "I swear, if she had anything to do with my mama getting killed…'

"We go to the police and let them handle her." Terrell cut me off. "Don't get yo hands dirty." I nodded. "Besides, do you really think she could've had something to do with it? You said they grew up together. Why would she want your mama dead?" I shrugged my shoulders and shook my head.

"I don't know. But if she did, I promise I'mma find out."

***

Once we unloaded the boxes at his house, Terrell took me to see his great grandparents. He led me down a long hallway to a massive room where they sat like a king and queen in their castle. Gold accented different shades of red, much like most of the house. They sat on an overstuffed couch looking at the news and I had to stifle my laughter. It was actually very pleasing to see a couple so far in their years still looking good and healthy and able to sit up and watch television.

"I want you to meet somebody." Terrell took my hand and pulled me between the couple and the television. "This is JaLea, my girlfriend." I waited nervously while they sized me up.

"She's pretty," the elderly man said to Terrell.

"Yes, she's very pretty," the woman countered. "Smart?" she asked Terrell.

"Yes," he answered quickly. "We study together all the time."

"I bet that's not all they do…"

"Charles, please!" the woman cut him off.

"I was just having some fun with the kids, Etta." I forced myself not to start cracking up in front of Terrell's great grandparents. I put my head down while Terrell laughed out loud.

"Yeah, okay, Pop." Terrell said.

"You're a very beautiful girl," Etta started. "You take care of my baby boy."

"Thank you. I will." I was amazed walking out of their room. We turned a corner where a huge elephant ear plant sat to the right. Terrell stopped short.

"You can close your mouth now." I had to laugh because I noticed I was still walking around in awe.

"First of all, are you sure those are your *great* grandparents?" He nodded and I shook my head. "Second of all… you kept a *big* secret from me."

"What secret?" He seemed genuinely confused.

"You're *RICH*! You are *loaded*!" He had the nerve to shake his head and keep walking. I followed rambling on with every step. "Have you *seen* your house?! Are we going back to your room? This ain't even the way we came." He was laughing at me but I still couldn't believe it. "You know what, I was thinking that your family had a lil' cash. I figured maybe that was why you could afford a brand new car, but I didn't wanna be nosy. Now I know. You're great grandparents are pushin' eighty and *still* livin' lavish! Did they rob banks or somethin'?" I joked.

We had finally made it back to his room when he

decided to answer. "They have shares in Microsoft and my great grandfather owns a McDonald's franchise and the Ford Motors down on Gravois." I plopped on the bed with a grin on my face that I knew looked dumb, but I couldn't help it. "I don't talk about it because I don't want people to use me or kick it with me just because I got money. I'm comfortable with you though so I guess I can tell you… I'm pretty much set for life."

"That's wild as hell. I don't wanna be nosy but I'm just really curious. How much are you worth?" There was a pause and Terrell's face twisted a little. "Never mind, I was outta line. You just…"

"Twenty-three million." I wanted to rip his clothes off and ride him right there in his ridiculously huge bedroom. He saw the look on my face and grinned like he could read my mind. "Come here," he ordered. I felt silly but got up anyway.

"So you mean to tell me you never used all that money to bribe anybody?"

"Ain't got it in me." I believed him and dropped to my knees in front of his open jeans.

***

"You think they heard us?" I asked Terrell after I pulled my shirt back on.

"Are you serious? We're kinda far away from them and they probably wouldn't know what was going on if they did hear."

"I wouldn't be so sure of that." I slid down on the thick, grey carpet and grabbed a box. Terrell sat beside me and did the same. I laughed as I pulled out polaroids from my mama's childhood and read the backs. *Me and my girls; My Baby Daddy, Aaron; Kickin' It…* Stacks of photos were stuffed in shoeboxes but I went back to the first picture I pulled out, *Me and My Girls*. I recognized mama and Tasha in an instant. The third girl looked vaguely familiar and I flipped through other photos, frantically trying to find her again.

"What's wrong, babe?" Terrell asked. I handed him the first picture along with another shoebox.

"Look at this girl and see if you can find…" Before I got the words out I found another picture with her name on the back. "Theresa!"

"That's crazy. It's really a small world." Terrell stared at the picture in his hands.

"What?" I asked him.

"Theresa… that's my mama."

THIRTY-EIGHT

I took the picture from him and held it up to his face studying them both. "Hmm, you don't look like her." Something in my gut was bothering me.

"What's wrong? It's not like it's a big deal. St. Louis is small and you stay pretty close. They probably went to the same school or something."

"Yeah, probably." I put the picture in my back pocket, debating on asking Tasha about her. "We should keep looking through these pictures."

"You really think you'll find somebody else you recognize? These are pretty old. They look younger than us on these pictures."

"I just wanna make sure I look at everything." I flipped through a few more photos and felt a jerk in my stomach.

Remember me bitch? Bet you never expected to see my face again! Left me in a gotdamn alley to die! Learned a good lesson didn't you?

I had blocked the words out until that moment. The movie had always played silently in my mind, but seeing his eyes, young but just as piercing, sent me back to that night. My mind was in shambles. Had my father been innocent all this time? Had my mother tried to *kill* somebody? If she did, it must've been with good reason. *What the hell?* It felt like I was losing my mind until I felt Terrell's hand on my shoulder.

"JaLea! What's wrong?" I snapped out of it.

"Find his name! I need his name!" I shoved the picture at Terrell. Before long he had found what I needed.

"Chris. His name is Chris Merritt." He handed me a small stack of about ten pictures. There was my mama, young, smiling, and happy, with her murderer. I turned each one over to read the disgusting antics on the backs. *Me and my Boo at the park; the Merritts; Kyra and Chris Merritt...* I felt sick.

"JaLea, you gotta tell me what's going on." I had almost forgotten I was sitting there in Terrell's room.

"This is the dude that killed my mama!!." He took the pictures from me, starring at each one.

"Baby, are you sure? They're pretty young on these pictures."

"If you had seen what I saw that night, you'd be able to spot him from a mile away." Understanding came over Terrell's face and he scooted behind me to rub my back.

"It's okay JaLea. If you're sure it's him, I'll do whatever I can to help you catch his ass." It was almost as if he could feel the anger boiling in my blood because he pulled away and took the pictures. "Let's finish up these last couple of boxes."

"Why?" I asked on the verge of tears. "We already know who to look for."

"Don't you wanna know why? Or how she even came in contact with him after all those years. She's gotta be what, thirteen on these pictures. What happened that he did that to her after they were grown?"

"I think she tried to kill him."

"*Kill* him!? JaLea are you sure?"

"Do you really think I'd say something like that about my mama if I didn't think it was true?" I replayed the horrific night for him, filling in the things that had been hiding in my selective memory.

"That dude had to know yall were gone be there. It's too much of a coincidence."

"As far as I know, only our cousins in Atlanta... and Tasha." Terrell looked back to his box.

"Why don't you stay here with me tonight? You shouldn't be alone." He knew what I was thinking. If Tasha was in front of me at that moment, I would've tried to stomp her face in the floor.

"That bitch is the only link." I ran down a list of people. "Grandma had no idea we were even in St. Louis until after everything went down, and mama wasn't trying to deal with my daddy. I couldn't even say goodbye to him so I know she didn't want him to know we were back. And my cousins been in Atlanta for as long as I can remember. I don't even think they knew Chris. But my mama grew up in St. Louis with Tasha. She would've known Chris when they were together."

"I think I found something." I looked over at Terrell, irritated, wondering if he had even been listening to me. The feeling subsided when I saw what he'd pulled out of the box. My heart thumped out of control watching him pull the rubber band off the rolled up notebook. It was purple, my mama's favorite color, with her maiden name, Kyra Blasik, written on the front with permanent marker. He handed me the book and I took it cautiously, not sure of what I might find. It took a minute to realize the picture of the fat baby she'd taped to the inside cover was me, smiling, nothing but gums. My eyes welled up with tears.

"You wanna take a break?" Terrell wiped my eyes and I was reluctant to put the book up but eager to go out with Terrell, knowing I really did need a break. He smiled and won me over. *Damn dimples!*

I waited patiently for Terrell to change and prayed that Tasha wasn't home so I could change in peace. Thankfully she wasn't.

***

After stuffing ourselves at Red Lobster, Terrell drove us to Tower Grove Park and laid out a comforter so we could lounge under an enormous tree. The night sky looked almost like it had back at school where the pollution was slim to none and every star was visible. The leaves above us rustled just a little from the November breeze and the serenity of the atmosphere blocked out the traffic on the nearby street. Dimly lit street lights painted haunting pictures on the grassy canvas beneath us.

"It's really crazy that our mama's used to kick it and now we hooked up," Terrell broke the silence.

"I wonder if they knew each other when they were pregnant with us," I added.

"I wonder if we took baths together when we were little," he said. I laughed and punched his arm.

"Seriously though, Terrell. I wonder why they fell out. They looked like they were real cool right around the time we woulda been born but I don't know her. Never met her or even heard of her."

"Yeah, something must've happened," he said. "But enough about that. Right now, it's about us." He bent down and hovered two inches from my face, smiling, before kissing me. We kissed for what seemed like hours, then his hand slid up my shirt. He ran his fingers across my bra before rolling me over on my side to unclasp the back. As I settled back on the cover, he gripped my breast with a roughness that made me moan. Then he slid his way down the comforter to the elastic hem of my skirt and traced my waist line with his tongue. He tugged on the sides of my skirt and I arched my back so he could get it down. I kept telling myself that it was late so hopefully no one would really be in the park, but all thoughts left my mind when Terrell pulled my thong to the side. I gasped when the cool air hit me and then again when his warm tongue slid between my legs. Excitement and fear gripped me. I wanted to make Terrell stop but I couldn't. I wanted to take all he was willing to give.

After he sent pleasure seizures through me, I had to beg him to stop. Laughing, he picked me up and carried me back to the car. We didn't leave the park for two hours.

***

Terrell insisted I load my suitcase in his trunk so we headed straight to his house from the park. I was skeptical at first about staying with him, but he assured me that his grandparents wouldn't mind, and probably wouldn't know I was there anyway. I tried to listen to his conversation on the drive back, but my mind kept wandering to that purple notebook. It could've been anything from a diary to school notes. So when Terrell went for his shower, I grabbed the notebook and settled in at his desk. Eager to look in the window to my mother's childhood, I cracked open the pages.

> *July 2, 1990*
> *I got away with something yesterday. I know I was wrong and I'm probably going to hell but the bastard deserved it. Matter of fact, I did him a favor. If I had called the police, he woulda been somebody's bitch, hopefully for the rest of his life. That's what I shoulda done. Let HIM find out how it feels to have somebody force a dick down his throat or up HIS ass! Let him see what he put me through everyday! My own damn daddy! But NO!! My dumb ass had to kill him! How stupid am I?*

I almost dropped the notebook. I had always wondered why I'd never heard two words about my grandfather. He raped my mama and she'd killed him for it. My mama *killed* her father. *My mama killed her father!* There was a part of me that was proud, but I was confused and had too many questions. What the hell was wrong with that man! How long had he been raping my mama? What did my grandma do about it?

"I started you some water." Terrell was standing in the doorway to the bathroom in nothing but a towel. The distinct grooves between each ab were still a little wet. Had it been fifteen minutes earlier, I would've ripped the towel off, but my mind was on the purple notebook. "I sat out soap and towels too."

"Thank you." I got up and headed for the bathroom door hoping he wouldn't try anything. I wasn't in the mood.

"You're taking the notebook with you?" I hadn't even realized I was clutching it in my armpit.

"Girls read in the tub." He shrugged with a 'yeah, okay' look and I forced a smile.

THIRTY-NINE

Terrell's bathroom was a kaleidoscope of blues with steps that led up to the enormous jacuzzi tub. It was masculine and sexy, and I thought for a split second about inviting him in, but I remembered the notebook. I quickly undressed, eased down into the soothing water, and began reading again. I held back tears as mama went on for the next three pages about how she and my daddy met, how she felt about him, how bad she wanted to be with him and how she was scared to approach him. When she started talking about them hooking up, I scanned through to the next entry.

> *July 10, 1990*
> *I'm being punished. GOD is driving me crazy and ruining my life for what I did. Kim is in the hospital with a 20% chance to live. Tasha tried to kill herself because of it. I wouldn't be able to forgive myself if Kim dies. She's Tasha's only sister and I love her like a sister and they're getting hurt to punish me.*

I leaned my head back against the rim of the tub. I didn't know a 'Kim'. I hadn't even known Tasha had a sister. Mama had never mentioned her just like she had never mentioned her friend Theresa. I wasn't surprised to read that Tasha had tried to commit suicide. The fact that her sister was on her death bed was enough to push anyone over the edge.

> *When I left the hospital from seeing Kim, I coulda sworn I saw my daddy on the bus. GOD was telling me it was my fault Kim fell on that glass. Then my dad tried to kill me in the tub. He tried to drown me and I know it was real but I feel like I'm going crazy or some shit. I know what I saw and I know what I felt and I know I killed his ass. I stabbed him right in the damn chest! And the bastard wants to take me down with him!*
>
> *I broke up with Reggie today and told him I wanted to be with Aaron and he tried to fight me! I swear, some niggas and they egos! And I had the nerve to run into Chris's ass!*

I inhaled involuntarily at the mention of *his* name. I didn't have his picture with me, but his face was engraved in my memory. I read on, cringing at the gory details of what happened the night Chris tried to rape my mama. Anger engulfed my soul and I tried to connect the dots between that night and the night of the murder. There was no way they would've talked after that. Did he track her down just to pay her back for biting him? He *did* claim she tried to kill him. It didn't make good sense to me that he'd hold such a grudge for over sixteen years, but who knows what's on any insane person's mind?

I was getting a headache and my water was getting cold. I hadn't lifted a finger to clean myself but I'd been soaking a good half hour. The chill hit me once I got out, so I dried off quickly and let the water out of the tub. Terrell was sound asleep when I stepped in the room with my towel on. I was hesitant at first. I'd never slept in a bed with anybody but my parents, and it had been years since I'd done that. I had agreed to stay over though, so I slid into my night clothes and eased under the covers, careful not to wake him. The sex was firre, but I had to finish my mama's diary before I shut my eyes.

> *I had to see Aaron. If I could lean on anybody, it would be him. But I go to knock on his window and who do I see his trifling' ass laid up with??? That ho THERESA!! The way I felt I coulda killed both they asses! I still can't believe it! Why would she want him after I been with him? After she knew how I felt? And why the hell didn't he get wit Theresa if he wanted her in the first damn place?! Why even play with my mind like that? FUCK BOTH OF EM! If that's what they want they can have each other. FUCK BOTH OF EM! All I need is me, myself and I.*

I looked over at a sleeping Terrell, trying not to fault him for what his mother did almost twenty years ago. My conscience was screaming, "His mama slept with your daddy! Get the hell outta there! I don't care if you have to walk!" I ignored it. I couldn't possibly be upset with Terrell for something that happened when he wasn't even thought of. I wanted so bad to wake him and tell him what I read about his mother. I knew I would've felt like crap if I let him read my mama's diary, but how could I come out and say, "Your mama was a ho." I kept reading.

> *July 29, 1990*
> *I CAN'T BELIEVE I'M PREGNANT!! With everything else messed up in my life WHY did my stupid ass have to get pregnant. I'M 15!?*

I read on, finding myself more and more disgusted with my mama. Knowing that, at one point, my mama didn't want me broke my heart. Knowing that I could've possibly been the product of incest... a pedophile and a rapist at that... rocked me to the core. To be completely honest, thinking about her situation, I would've wanted an abortion too.

By three in the morning, my eyes were worn out and I was starting to feel like I was just being nosy. After reading that Chris got locked up, I was almost certain that when he got out he went looking for my mama. There was really no reason to go on reading, but I couldn't stop myself. I glanced over at Terrell who was stirring peacefully in his sleep. I wondered if he knew the real reason why he had to live with his mother's grandparents who gave him money instead of love. Did he know his mother shook him and his grandmother was too busy to care? I ran my fingers through his curls, unable to imagine what it would've been like to grow up the way he did, like the rich kids in the movies who would trade in their cash for a loving parent. I figured his great grandparents did the best they could though. They didn't have to take care of him in the first place but they had taken him in and set him up for life.

Oct. 30, 1991

> *God please calm my nerves. I want Theresa dead more than I did my child molesting daddy! She's lucky the police came when they did or I would've done more than punch the bitch in her face. I never met anybody with balls big enough to take somebody's child right form under their nose.*

I read on, confused and enraged. Terrell's mother understandably had it out for my mama but *damn*! She was just flat out crazy. Why hadn't I known? Why hadn't anyone ever said anything to me about being kidnapped? I tried to see things from my parents' point of view. What would've been the point in telling me? I could see Terrell's great grandparents sweeping the whole incident under the rug just like my parents had. How could they possibly tell him what a monster his mother was? Terrell was sweet, funny, smart and fine as hell. How could he have come from a woman like Theresa? Just then, something started nagging at me, something I hadn't caught before. I flipped through the pages until I caught it.

> *I guess Theresa's ass thought she could get brownie points since she never slept with Reggie. But her dumb ass still got played by Aaron's uncle. That's what the hell she get for tryin so hard to get MY man! Now she got a baby by a man almost twice her age. Marcus don't want her or that baby.*

If all that was true about who Terrell's father was, then I had lost my virginity to my gotdamn cousin!

FORTY

"Baby, what's going on?" Terrell rolled over when I accidentally bumped into his dresser pulling my clothes on.

"This cannot be real!"

"What?"

"How did my life end up a damn Keisha Ervin novel?!"

"*What* are you talkin' about?" Terrell rubbed his eyes and started to get up.

"No! You stay right the hell there! All of this… *everything* is… *wrong*. I gotta get outta here." Terrell was baffled and looked around the room aimlessly until he focused on the purple notebook.

"What does that notebook say?" I didn't skip a beat pulling my tennis shoes on. I jumped up when he reached for the book but I was too slow. "I'm not gone read it but you *are* gone tell me why you were about to sneak out of here at damn near five in the morning without even a *bye Terrell*." I hesitated. He said he wouldn't read the book, but I knew he wouldn't give it back to me if I didn't start talking.

"I know your father." Time stood still. I'd only met my uncle Marcus a handful of times. It had been years since I'd last seen him, but Terrell had the curls and hazel eyes. My hazel eyes, my father's hazel eyes…

"What are you talking about? What do you mean you

know my father? *I* don't even know my father." He was coming toward me and the look in his eyes scared me. I swallowed hard before continuing. He deserved to know what we were to each other.

"Our mother's used to be best friends so they pretty much knew the same people. Your mom met your dad through my father." I stopped there but Terrell wasn't buying it.

"So what? That's no reason for you to jet outta here like this. What's going on, JaLea?"

"Your father is a lot older than your mom and they were in this on and off relationship I guess, but he didn't really want..."

"Stop bullshittin' me and tell me what's up!" For a split second, I wanted to jump down Terrell's throat for cursing me out, but he was right. I *was* bullshittin' him. I was scared of the outcome. I was crazy about him but for us to be together, we'd just be continuing our family's crazy saga.

"Your father is my uncle." I watched his facial expression twist into something I couldn't read. What was he thinking?

"Don't play games JaLea. That shit ain't cute. If you wanna leave don't make up stories."

"Your father is my father's uncle." We stared at each other, caught in a web of confusion and disbelief. My head was pounding. Reading my mama's diary was like reading a juicy novel starring all the people in my life. It was non-fiction, raw and uncensored. Rape and murder ran through my veins. And I had the same blood as the first man I ever held my heart out to. My mind was a tornado of chaos as I fought back tears. My body was torn between Terrell and the door. He was the only person left in my life that I could lean on and I couldn't even do that. He was the only person I'd ever opened up to, given myself to and let into the darkest corner of my memory. But all his secrets played a major part in my life. He had no idea the torment his mother had put mine through. And most of all, he was my *cousin*!

"I have to go." I bent over to grab the handle of my suitcase, giving Terrell enough time to block the door.

"Where are you going?"

"Home. Where else?' I tried to sound irritated when, in reality, I was hoping he'd beg me to stay.

"Look, I know this seems like a messed up situation--"

"*Seems* like!" I cut him off.

"Listen. I'm not sure I really believe it. I wanna be with you and until you can prove this mess to me…"

"It's all in the book--" He sat the notebook on his bed and came to me.

"I'm not trying to call your mom a lie. Believe that. I just wanna get to the bottom of this." He put his hands on my shoulders sending shivers down to my toes. *Damn!* Why did he have to touch me? "This is strange as hell, I know that. So if you really wanna leave I won't make you stay. But you're not walking home." He yanked his pullover off the back of a chair and pulled on his tennis shoes.

The ride was quiet and filled with tension. I figured Terrell didn't know what to say. I sure didn't. I'd dropped a hell of a bomb on him and he was trying to digest things just as I was. He was in denial, but I knew the truth.

We pulled up to the house to find the living room light on. I looked at the clock on the dash and it read 5:23 a.m. What was she doing up so early?

"You sure you wanna stay here?" Terrell cut the engine. Before I could answer, I saw two figures moving through the living room.

"Come with me." I whispered to Terrell as if the shadows in the house could hear me.

"What are we doing?" he asked tip toeing after me through the gangway.

"Eavesdropping," I answered, crouching down under a living room window. I searched for a stick and when I found a useful one I wedged it under the window pane. I strained for what seemed like forever until the window gave way and creaked open.

"I was stupid enough to think you really wanted to see me. I told you I didn't want any part of this!" a female voice screamed.

"Kim *please*." I recognized Tasha begging. "I don't have anybody else. You know I can't talk to anybody else."

"You think I wanted to know what you did! You should've kept that shit to yourself!" Kim yelled back at her.

"What did she do? Come on, *say it*." I whispered.

"You know it was either me or her. I had no choice." I force myself to stay crouched on the ground. There was no doubt in my mind that they were talking about my mama, but I needed specifics. "Jalea took some of her boxes from the basement. What if she finds something!?" Tasha was panicking.

"Honestly, I hope she does. But Kyra had no idea what was going on so I'm sure there's nothing in her stuff that points to you." I eased up a little to peek through a slit in the curtains. Tasha plopped down on the couch looking defeated. Her sister was facing her, arms crossed, so I couldn't see her face. "You know, if JaLea is anything like her mom, she's figured it out by now." Tasha jerked towards Kim.

"What do you mean? She's been here for two years. I love her like a daughter."

"I'm not saying you don't. But the night you set Kyra up, you set yourself up to." I felt like punching the bricks of the window sill. My blood ran hot and I jumped up but Terrell caught my waist and held me against his chest.

"This is what you wanted right?" he whispered. "Don't you wanna find out why?"

"Let me see your phone." Terrell hesitated but handed

me his cell.

"How did you I set myself up?" The conversation continued inside.

"Don't be stupid, Tasha. You're the *only* one who knew Kyra would be back in St. Louis. You even told her and JaLea someone had been driving around the house. Did you think Chris was joking?" I froze. I even felt Terrell tense up behind me. I almost forgot about the phone in my hand.

"9-1-1! What's your emergency?!" I guess the operator had had to repeat herself because she was hollering into the phone.

"I have information about a murder, the Kyra Washington case." Terrell nudged me and I pushed his hand away. I couldn't go another minute knowing all I knew.

"You're gonna have to come down to the police station and fill out--"

"I can't leave!" The loud whisper scared me. I didn't want Tasha or Kim to hear me. "I'm listening to a confession *right now* and if the police don't get here then a witness could be gone." Reluctantly, the operator took my information and agreed to dispatch a car to the house. "What did I miss?' I asked, lifting back up to peek in the window.

"Tasha started crying." Terrell replied. I smiled a little and listened closely.

"I never meant for this to happen…"

"You never meant for this to happen my ass!" Kim finally turned and, even though I was dying to see her face, Terrell and I scrambled to get down for fear of being caught. "Chris stopped you outside Kyra's house and beat the hell outta you to find out where she was. Put you in the *hospital*. And you didn't even do anything to him. What do you think he wanted Kyra back in St. Louis for, to rekindle a silly little pre-teen relationship?"

"I wasn't thinking."

"You were thinking good enough to lie to get her down here. How do you think she felt? You made her believe you got beat up because she ran. You knew she'd come back here to pay that money and you knew Chris would be here waiting for her!" My eyes darted back and forth between the partially open window and the street. It had only been a couple of minutes but I was getting impatient waiting on the police. "Where is the money anyway, Tasha?"

"The police took it out the car when they searched it, *Kim*." Tasha huffed like she was offended at the fact that she was being accused of not only setting my mama up but stealing money too. "I don't know what else to say. I just really need your help."

"What do you want *me* to do? What am I supposed to do to keep JaLea from figuring out the truth if she hasn't already? I won't rat you out but if it comes to it, I won't put myself in the line of fire lying for you. You're my sister and I love you but that was *your* bad decision. Your stupid ass, bad decision that cost your best friend her life."

"What was I supposed to do?" Tasha jumped up from the couch with her arms out at her sides. The desperation on her face was beautiful. The police were on their way and I prayed Kim would stand her ground. "What would you have done?"

"I would've called the police after I got my ass beat. That thought didn't cross your mind? You didn't even give Kyra a chance." Tasha stood there looking simple minded. I wanted to bust her right then and there, tell her I heard everything... and then beat her into the ground. I wanted to take every ounce of frustration that had built up over the past two years and let it out with my fists slamming against her face. I wanted to stomp her for my grandma. She was laying up in a convalescent home unable to take care of herself because she couldn't deal with losing her only child.

A switch flipped in my brain. I was living my nightmare

again. Mama was walking to her car and I saw the man coming up the driveway, but I couldn't get there fast enough. The shots rang out and I couldn't control my screams. My throat had begun to hurt when Tasha and Kim came out to see what was going on.

"JaLea! What the hell?" If Terrell hadn't had a grip around my waist I would've ran up the porch and tackled her. Kim, an older version of Tasha, was dumbfounded as I yelled obscenities at her sister. I had all but passed out in Terrell's arms by the time the police car finally pulled up.

FORTY-ONE

Kim sat in the waiting area of the police station with Terrell and me. I wanted so desperately to listen to Tasha through the two way mirror, but I was lucky the officers didn't haul me to the hospital psych ward instead. It had taken two of the to get me to shut up.

"Don't worry, she's finally backed into a corner so she'll crack and tell them the truth," Kim reassured. "Besides, she knows I'm going to tell them anyway. I've kept this inside for too long." I sat there looking at her not knowing what to feel. Even though she didn't know me, she knew I was staying with someone who was partly responsible for my mother's murder. For almost two years one of the main reasons I hated my father was the fact that I thought he was to blame for what happened to my mama. For almost two years I was obedient and put up with all Tasha's crap when her ass should've been in jail. I looked at Kim wondering if I should hate her too, but at that point I was numb.

"Why haven't I met you before?" I waited, surprisingly patient, and Terrell slipped his arms around my shoulders to comfort me.

"I had an... accident when I was pregnant." I still clutched the purple notebook in my hand and I knew she was talking about when she fell on the glass. "Tasha went through severe depression and, after I had my son, so did I. My family, including Tasha, wanted to believe we were picture perfect. I couldn't take it. I had to leave St. Louis." For a moment, I regretted asking her. I didn't feel like listening to her sob story. I had my own.

"So you didn't keep in touch, not even with your parents?" I was setting her up, trying to see if she was lying.

"I talked to my parents probably twice a month. Maybe more. Tasha and I talked every blue moon. She hated me for leaving. One day she called from the hospital. Your mom's ex had beat her up pretty good trying to find out where you two were. When he found out you weren't even in St. Louis anymore, he told Tasha to get your mom back here. But instead of telling her the truth, Tasha told your mom that your father beat her up and some man threatened her about money your dad owed. She knew your mom would come back to help her."

"How did he know where we would be?" I gripped Terrell's hand remembering Tasha's words. *It was either her or me. I had no choice.*

"She told him where she lives."

"This is the dumbest thing I ever heard." Kim and I both turned to look at Terrell. "For one, she could've told police what was goin' down when they took her to the hospital. She could've told your mom the truth to turn that shit around him. She could've given him the wrong address. *Anything*!"

"All I know is what she told me. She called me again that night crying. She needed somebody to talk to, so I listened. She felt so bad, I thought she'd turn herself in, but she never did. I was shocked as hell when she told me you moved in with her." It wasn't until that moment I realized I didn't have anywhere to go. Sure, I could track down some distant cousin like mama had done. Then I'd have to relocate, *again*. The police station walls were closing in on me and I felt the old JaLea resurfacing. Shy, quiet and unsure of herself. Then Terrell kissed my forehead and I leaned into him. Being in his arms at that moment was bittersweet. I needed him and he was there for me, but what we wanted was unthinkable. I had to figure out a way to break free of him. My heart was in enough trouble already.

"Miss Washington, they're ready for you." I stood up when the officer came for me.

"Can he come in?" I motioned towards Terrell and the officer nodded hesitantly.

With Terrell holding my hand, I drained my memory bank, once again reliving the pain of a father on drugs and the murder of my mother. When it was all over, they made me hand over the purple notebook. I did, almost happily. I'd had my fair share of breakthroughs for one night.

As Terrell and I were on our way out, they were taking Kim in. She gave me a weak smile and squeezed my shoulder. I could only pray that she'd tell the truth just as she told me. Even though they were estranged, I knew it had to be hard as hell to turn in your sister. Terrell put his arm around me and I thought about my own parents years ago in the same police station dealing with their own drama. That incident brought them closer and marked the beginning of their relationship. I looked up at Terrell feeling the anguish in my chest, knowing that we could never be them. Not even close.

"I'm taking you back to my house," his voice boomed with a masculine forcefulness I couldn't argue with.

***

I woke to the smell of turkey and dressing and sat up in the bed. When we got back to his house in the wee hours of the morning, Terrell had insisted that I take the bed and he make a pallet on the floor. Rubbing my eyes, I saw that he had already folded his pallet and was sitting at the computer. The clock on the desk read 11:22 a.m. "Did they start cooking for Thanksgiving already?" I asked, suddenly terrified. I knew his great grandparents weren't cooking so there had to be other members of his family there.

"Yeah, they are." His voice was low and monotonous.

"What's wrong?" I asked making the bed.

"My mama's down there." I continued making the bed, unable to stop my chest from heaving. I'd almost forgotten about things I had read about her. There was a feeling I could only describe as a fiery hatred in my gut. I needed to see her. I needed her to look into my eyes and feel my pain. At the same time, it felt like I was betraying Terrell. I couldn't sort out all the emotions swirling around in my head. With Terrell, I had a passion and excitement that was new and addictive. It was something I had to learn to live without, not only because of who his father was, but because of his mother too. Amazingly, I felt the same negative pull towards Terrell's mother as I did Tasha, and I hadn't even met the woman.

"Okay well I'll get dressed. I know other people are down there. It'll be better than bein' cooped up in your room smellin' food all day." He just nodded.

Once in the bathroom, I panicked. I was about to meet Terrell's mother. *Theresa.* The woman who kidnapped me, slept with my father *and* shook her baby. After I showered, I stared at my reflection feeling silly. Theresa was a young girl when those things happened. A teenager who felt betrayed and obviously needed all the help she could get. There was no telling if jail had hurt or helped her. Either way, I wasn't about to act a fool, disrespect Terrell, or ruin Thanksgiving over something that happened years ago.

After Terrell got dressed, I followed him through the massive halls, captivated by his Hugo Boss. The scent took me back to the night in the park. His broad shoulders flexed under his t-shirt and I took a deep breath remembering how he'd picked me up and carried me back to the car.

"You okay, JaLea?" Terrell was talking to me and all I could do was nod and give a phony grin.

The aromas engulfed me as we rounded the hall to the busy kitchen. The talking and laughing in between chopping and mixing almost depressed me. It had been so long since I had family get together like that. Terrell whisked me quickly through the hustle and bustle, giving short introductions so we could get back out of the way. I didn't remember half the people in the kitchen as he took my hand leading me towards the hall. At the entrance to the living room, my breath stopped short.

"You sure you wanna meet my mom? I mean we could go back upstairs and play cards or something." Terrell whispered. We stood there starring at the back of her head and what I figured was the back of her man's head by the way she was hanging all over him. "That's nasty. We should just go somewhere and chill or somethin'." I didn't wanna seem too eager, but I had to get him to introduce me. I'd already decided to keep my cool; I just needed to see the woman face to face. She turned around abruptly and I almost hyperventilated.

Her hair was pulled back in a tight, full ponytail, easily showing off the bags under her red eyes. She was a deep almond brown with high cheek bones, and when she smiled I could see the wear and tear that the drugs had taken on her teeth. Strangely though, I could tell how at one time she'd been the pretty girl in the pictures with my mama.

"Hey sweetie!" She jumped up to give Terrell a hug and, as she did, her friend turned and my heart sunk to the floor. My voice came out in a diminutive whisper.

"Daddy?"

I hadn't been able to put my finger on it until I saw my father sitting there on the couch. The girl he had cheated on my mama with when they were teenagers was the same damn crack head that he cheated on her with when they were grown and married. The same bitch he brought to my mama's *funeral*. The same hoe that *kidnapped* me!

"*That's* your pops?!" Terrell was as dumbfounded as the rest of us.

"Hi JaLea, it's nice to finally meet you." Theresa extended her hand and I wanted to spit on it.

"*We've met before.*" I managed to say.

"Hey, baby." My father was *not* happy to see me. "What are you doing here?"

"I was invited to spend Thanksgiving here. I guess I don't have to ask what *you're* doing here… with her." I jerked my head toward Theresa.

"Wait a minute, wait a minute. Am I missin' somethin'. I thought you didn't know my mama!" Terrell yelled. Theresa, my father and I stood quietly, neither of us wanting to divulge secrets that could send the room spinning.

"You need to talk to yo' mama," I told Terrell. I grabbed my father's hand and pulled him out the room and up the hall until I was sure Terrell couldn't hear. "How could you do this to my mama?" I wanted to slap him. Not only was he there with that… *woman*, but he looked like hell run over… twice.

"This is complicated, grown-up stuff…"

"Stop with the b.s.! I don't wanna hear it! I wanna know how you could lay up with her after everything that happened. You're worse than she is." He stood there with his mouth hanging open, seemingly unable to comprehend what was going on. "I found mama's diary." He closed his eyes exhaled long and slow. "Yeah, bet you didn't even know she had one. I know *everything*. Mind telling me how you hooked up with her *again*? After she kidnapped me! Don't you feel nasty being with somebody that had a baby with yo' uncle?"

"First of all, all that you sayin', that was a long time ago." I heard footsteps behind us and turned to see Terrell and his mother.

"She told me she tried to *kidnap* you! She said it like it wasn't nothin'!" He looked at my father then, as if asking the same question I was awaiting the answer to.

"I guess you remember what was going on before I moved out." *No shit Sherlock.* "I was in a really bad place in my life and Theresa was part of that."

"Okay so you expect me to believe you're not still with her." I was getting more and more disgusted with him.

"We're good friends, that's all. And Terrell's father isn't my uncle. Marcus is just a good friend too, like Tasha is… was with your mama."

"*Tasha was* not *my mama's friend!!*" I pushed past him, turning up a hall that looked much like all the others. The footsteps behind me quickened until Hugo Boss wafted through my nostrils and Terrell grabbed my arm.

"You okay?" he asked.

"Yeah, he just pissed me off. No disrespect, but why the hell would he still wanna be with her?"

"No disrespect, but crack heads do some off the wall stuff. I see it first hand." Before I could answer, Terrell pushed me up against the wall, kissing me with so much intensity I couldn't stop myself from reciprocating. Soon as he backed up I regretted it. "Don't look like that."

"How can I not? I just found my daddy with the woman who kidnapped me. Your mama came out and *told* you she kidnapped me and you wanna *kiss*!?" I was on the verge of tears from being horny and confused at the same time.

"I'm just tryin' to get yo' mind off all this. And by the way you acted, I guess you didn't hear what your pops said." I was stuck. I thought about everything that had been said, remembering the comment he made about Terrell's father being a friend, not an uncle. I was so upset by him calling Tasha my mama's *friend*, that I hadn't even paid attention. All it took was for me to grin at Terrell and he took me upstairs to celebrate.

***

Thanksgiving was like Christmas. I had a man who was romantic, intelligent, sexy, rich as hell, and *no relation* to me at all. I spent the holiday with a family that embraced me and made me feel like one of their own. My father and Terrell's mother stayed away, which kept the day pleasant. I loved my father simply because he was my father, but I decided I'd be cool with seeing him every blue moon. Terrell hadn't lied about his family's cooking. Everything tasted fantastic from the turkey and dressing and cranberry sauce to the greens, macaroni and cheese, sweet potatoes and dinner rolls. I was so stuffed I had to pass on the chocolate cake. Just when we made it to the corner before Terrell's room, his phone started ringing and he jogged sluggishly ahead to get it. Before I even made it to the room, he was rushing back out.

"They got a line up for you at the station." At that moment, I forgot how full and sleepy I was and Terrell and I raced to the car. Kim was pulling up to the station when we got out.

"They called you too?" I asked her.

"Yeah but I don't know why. Last time I saw Chris, he and your mom were kids."

Terrell put his arm around me as we waited for the officers to finish with Kim. It wasn't until she came out and shook one of the officer's hands that I got scared. I refused to be a punk, no matter how hard my heart was thumping against my ribcage.

"Chris was locked up when he was younger and they had me looking at some old mug shots to pick him out," she explained to me. "It was easier than I thought. Plus, this'll be his third strike." Kim winked at me and put my mind at ease a little. I knew I wouldn't be looking at mug shots though.

"Miss Washington, we're ready for you," an officer motioned towards the open door. Terrell popped up but I rose slowly.

"You can do this," he reassured me.

"You can, sweetie." Kim was beside me. "Put his ass away for your mama. He's had enough free time." And with that, I marched in like I owned the place.

"I'm going to show you six men," the officer stated.

"They will step up, speak their line and step back." I stood in the small room looking through the two-way mirror as the six men walked across the platform. They took their places and as soon as they turned, my heart did too.

Number five was looking into my soul, just as he had that night. "It's number five," I blurted out. The officer and the two lawyers in the room stopped short.

"Young lady, they haven't even said the line yet. Maybe you need more time." I knew that had to be Chris's lawyer. I guess the officer decided to ignore me and got right down to business. He pushed the intercom button.

"Say the line number one."

"Remember me, bitch? Left me in a gotdamn alley to die." I heard him but I wasn't listening. All six men were tall and thick with dark complexions and low hair cuts, but number five was *Christopher Merritt*. His eyes gave him away. They'd haunted my dreams since I was sixteen.

I played their little game and listened to all six men. When they finished, I looked dead into the eyes of the ignorant lawyer and repeated myself. "Its number *five*."

I wrote down my selection, making sure the word FIVE was big and bold, then I signed the proper paperwork and we left the station. There was a tremendous weight lifted off my shoulders as we got in the car.

"I can't believe what we did in less than a week." Terrell beamed. "We make a pretty good team, huh?" I smiled and kissed his cheek before we pulled off. He went on rambling, joking about CSI and Law and Order, but my mind was on my mama. I knew the paperwork still had to be put through the system but, between Tasha, Kim, myself and the purple notebook, my mama would soon be resting easy. I'd helped her fight her demons from the grave and I couldn't have been happier. It had been so long since I felt that way, and I was planning to ride it out to the end.

Read on for an excerpt from T.C. Flenoid's next book:

SCANDOLOUS

prologue

The drunk snatched her Patron off the table and put it to her lips, tipping the bottle up slowly. Once she felt the soothing burn in her chest, she sat the bottle back down, jumping at the loud *CLANK*! it made when it hit the glass. With the back of her shaky hand, she wiped away fresh tears mixed with two day old mascara. Her eyes, now merely slits in her face, scanned the room aimlessly, seeing nothing. Darkness engulfed the living room with the same intensity it had the past few months of her life.

The contents of the woman's drinking binge bubbled in her stomach. Her mind told her she needed to hurry up and get to the bathroom, but her body wouldn't obey. Even as the alcohol tunneled its way back out of her mouth like a faucet, she stayed on the floor, arms propped up on the seat of the couch behind her, legs stretched out under the coffee table. It took all of five minutes to pull herself up from the floor and she grimaced as vomit slid off her bare legs. Empty Hennessy, Vodka and Grey Goose bottles littered the floor and she stumbled over them on her way to the bathroom.

On the third try, she was able to get a grip on the light cord above the medicine cabinet. After hour upon hour of drinking, the brightness almost sent her into shock. It took a while for her eyes to adjust, but when they did, she was repulsed by her reflection. Her hair was tangled and all over her head, revealing bald spots, her jaw was swollen and bruises were scattered across her face. Her t-shirt, which, if she remembered correctly, used to be white, was torn and covered in blood and vomit. She shook her head at the sight and got an instant headache. Memories flooded her mind with waves of pain and guilt.

    In her delusional state, her face twisted and people in the mirror were laughing at her, pointing fingers, mocking her. "Shet up!" she yelled through drunken slurs. "Shet-da fuck-up!" . She brought her fist up and slammed it into the glass. Jagged cracks shot through the mirror and blood gushed from her knuckles.

    "Shit!" the woman screamed, grabbing her hand. She slowly trudged back to her bedroom, the throbbing pain bringing her down from her high. The sole window in the room was open and it called out to her. The November wind blasted through and the woman welcomed the sting against her wet shirt and bare legs. She was in a daze and never heard her front door creak open and click quietly shut. Never heard the intruder tiptoe over the empty bottles back to the bedroom where she was. She never even had a chance to save herself as the gloved hands shoved her out of her twelfth story window.